MATISSE

on the

loose

MATISSE

on the loose

a novel by

Georgia Bragg

DELACORTE PRESS

All rights reserved. Published in the United States by Delacorte Press,
an imprint of Random House Children's Books, a division of
Random House, Inc., New York.

Delacorte Press is a registered trademark and the colophon
is a trademark of Random House, Inc.

Visit us on the Web! www.randomhouse.com/kids

Educators and librarians, for a variety of teaching tools, visit us at
www.randomhouse.com/teachers

Library of Congress Cataloging-in-Publication Data
Bragg, Georgia.
Matisse on the loose / Georgia Bragg.—1st ed.
p. cm.
Summary: An aspiring artist's daily routine of being embarrassed by his
eccentric family is interrupted when he finds himself in the middle of an
art museum fiasco involving Matisse's 1909 portrait of his son Pierre.
ISBN 978-0-385-73570-4 (hardcover)—ISBN 978-0-385-90559-6 (library
binding)—ISBN 978-0-375-89262-2 (e-book) [1. Family life—Fiction.
2. Artists—Fiction. 3. Art museums—Fiction. 4. Museums—Fiction.
5. Matisse, Henri, 1869–1954. Portrait of Pierre Matisse—Fiction.
6. Humorous stories.] I. Title.
PZ7.B7326Mat 2009
[Fic]—dc22   2008019624

The text of this book is set in 12-point Century Book.
Book design by Trish Parcell Watts
Printed in the United States of America
10 9 8 7 6 5 4 3 2 1
First Edition

For Harvey,
Maisy,
and
Cody

Acknowledgments

I want to thank Edward Necarsulmer IV for completely changing my life.

This book couldn't have been written without the tireless support and good ideas of Camille Alick, Victoria Beck, Christine Bernardi, Laurie C. Lepik, Tracy Holczer, Leslie Margolis, Elizabeth Passarelli, Anne Reinhard, and Angela Wiencek.

Thank you to Donna Bragg for arranging the dots and dashes and everything else that makes a sentence sit up straight on a piece of paper.

A huge thanks to my mom and dad; they inspire me in every way, every day.

And I especially want to thank Wendy Loggia for giving me a chance.

1

My family is like the sun. It's dangerous to look right at them. You have to look at them through a little hole in a box.

For starters, Dad has his barbecue. It was specially made out of two oil drums welded together. Then Dad added the wheels with shock absorbers. It can hold a sixty-pound pig. He rolls the thing all the way to the butcher, half a mile away. The butcher balances a pig on the spit and then Dad wheels the porker home. He wheels it to pool parties, soccer games, and funerals—whatever—if someone's paying him, he'll be there. And with the wide-load flags sticking out of both sides of his barbecue, my dad is just one big advertisement for someone whose brains are all gone. No matter what direction he goes in, all the kids seem to find their way to the curb to see him, where they laugh so hard they cry.

I've avoided being seen anywhere near Dad's barbecue. I'd like to keep my regular eleven-year-old life going as long as possible and not join the ranks of the crazy people I live with. I am not above diving into bushes or crawling through a storm drain in the opposite direction. I haven't actually crawled through a storm drain, but I would if I had to. One time I jumped out of a moving car. Dad was pushing his barbecue down the road, and he was getting close to the mall where everybody from school hangs out. Mom and I were following him in the car. Kids started gathering on the sidewalk like they were waiting for the Rose Parade or something. So, before we got to the mall, where even more people would see me with him, I opened the car door, tucked into a ball, and threw myself into the street. It wasn't as hard as it sounds, since Mom was driving at about a quarter of a mile an hour.

Now Dad was at it again. A new Miss Piggy with her face still attached was freshly skewered and ready to roll. We were going to the Geraldine Emmett Art Museum, where Mom is the head of security, for their annual spring barbecue.

"Hey, Matisse, get my apron and chef's hat, would you, son?" Dad asked.

"Yeah, sure." I pulled Dad's gear out of the closet and stood at the kitchen counter watching him unlock the barbecue from the railing at the side of the house. He actually thinks someone might steal his rolling eyesore.

Mom wriggled my two-year-old brother, Man Ray, out of his swinging jumper thingy and slung him on her hip. She looked over at me, and I could tell what was coming. "So, Matisse, are you going to help Dad push the barbecue or come in the car with me?" she asked, even though she already knew the answer.

"With you," I said.

Mom waited a moment and then huffed, "You could go with Dad this once."

I might as well tattoo *nut job* on my forehead. "No, I'm going in the car," I insisted.

Mom walked toward the door, stopped at the bottom of the stairs, and called to my sister, "Frida, we're going now."

I followed Mom outside and jumped into the backseat of the car with Man Ray. Mom honked the horn and rolled down the window. "Frida!" she hollered. *Honk.* "We're going to be late." *Honk. Honk.*

Frida yanked back her purple curtains. "Hang on." My fourteen-year-old sister has a purple problem.

Everything she wears and everything she has in her room is purple, and if it were possible, everything she ate would be purple too. She finally appeared in a one-of-a-kind handmade outfit in a combination of lavenders and violets that made my eyes water.

Dad had maneuvered his double-wide barbecue out front. He threw his head back and smiled at Mom. "Are you ready, Sue-baby?"

"I'm ready, baby." Mom grinned as she drove behind Dad while he pushed the brown bomb right into the middle of the street.

There's only one way from our house to anywhere: go down a small hill and hang a left at the bottom out of our cul-de-sac.

As always, about fifteen seconds after push-off, Mom popped her head out the window and said to Dad, "I hope you brought your driver's license." Then, no surprise, Mom and Dad both laughed really hard, so hard it made me think their heads were full of clowns on little bicycles.

And that was my cue to duck down so that no one could see me. I leaned over and buried my head between my knees. I wasn't going to sit up again until we reached the museum. But then Mom screeched to a stop.

"Baby, are you all right?" Mom yelled out the window.

As I sat up, Mom and Frida jumped out of the car.

Dad was splayed out on the road with one leg bent up behind him. "Shoot," he said, "I think I sprained my ankle."

The three of us hoisted Dad off the pavement. We brushed him off and helped him hobble to the car. I was sorry Dad got hurt, but it sure seemed like a good excuse to leave the barbecue at home for once. When we were all back in our seats, we saw it: the barbecue was rattling its way down the hill all by itself.

Mom leaned hard on the horn. We caught up with the barbecue and hollered a few things back and forth to each other, but there was just nothing we could do to stop it. As the barbecue banged along, the hood jiggled open and the dead pig was swinging from side to side. It was the ugliest thing you've ever seen, all pink and bald.

It got worse. The dead pig was headed right for the Jeffersons' house.

The Jeffersons' front yard was full of kids celebrating Johnny Jefferson's fifth birthday. A big inflatable bouncer hogged most of the lawn.

The partygoers started screaming their heads off when they saw the pig coming right at them. Mr. Jefferson cleared everybody out of the way only about a second before sixty pounds of raw pork crashed into the bouncer. The pig's body smashed up against the mesh wall of the bouncer, which cut a checkerboard pattern into the pig's pink flesh. Nobody got hurt, but I could tell that was pretty much the end of the party.

Mom slammed on the brakes and everybody but me jumped out of the car—including Dad, who was hopping on one foot. I was fine, watching the crash scene, crouched down in the backseat.

Dad and Mr. Jefferson did some kind of secret handshake. They had a fathers-and-their-barbecues code-of-honor thing going. So Mr. Jefferson was happy to be promised a hunk of meat for all the trouble and to call it a day.

I watched Lizzie and Toby Jefferson comfort the birthday boy while his friends stared at the pig and then began running around playing freeze tag. Lizzie and Toby are in sixth grade with me. Toby is my best friend, but his twin sister, Lizzie, thinks I'm dumb and has made it her mission to prove it.

After the hoopla was over, Mom spotted me still in the car. "Matisse!" She flapped her arm around and around in the universal get-over-here motion.

I didn't have any choice but to get out and meet Mom and Frida on the sidewalk.

"Kids," Mom said. "Dad's pig needs to get squared up again on that pole thing and then pushed the rest of the way to the museum."

"I can't do it. I'm wearing sandals." Frida's purple toenails gripped her purple flip-flops.

"Matisse, it's you, then," Mom said.

"Mom. No way." It was about to happen—the one thing I'd hoped I'd never ever be stuck doing. "I am not going to push that thing down the street."

Mom grabbed my elbow. "Don't hurt your father's feelings," she whispered. "It's only four blocks away. It won't kill you."

"Are you sure about that?" I pointed at the runaway barbecue. "I'm not doing it."

Mom buzzed off across the yard and returned twenty seconds later with Toby in tow. "Listen, Toby," Mom said. "You are such a good friend to Matisse. Is there any way you could help us with something?"

"Sure."

"Help Matisse push his dad's barbecue to the art museum."

"There isn't a chance in—" Toby started, but stopped when I whacked him on the arm. There was no telling what Toby would say since he's lacking the hey-maybe-I-shouldn't-say-that interceptor gland. "Oh." Toby looked at me, then back at Mom. "I might be busy."

"He can't do it," I told her.

"Toby. Pleeeeease. Pleeeeease." Mom was about to get down on her knees.

"Oh jeez." Toby saw what was coming. If my mom wants you to do something, you're doing it before you even know what hit you. "All right, I'll do it."

"Fabulous." Mom and everybody headed back to the car. "Okay, boys, take the bull by the horns. Let's go."

"Oh yes! Oh baby, this should be good." Lizzie spun around in a big hurry and ran into the house.

"You don't have to help me," I told Toby. It really was a lot to ask of a friend. "I wouldn't do it either if I were you."

"Look," Toby said, "I'll help you get it back on its wheels, but that's it. I've got to think about my reputation."

"Let's just get it over with."

It took all our muscles to get the hunk of bacon straightened out. The rubbery pigskin was hard to hang on to, and the grill slid completely out from under the pig when we lost our grip swinging it back into place. We finally got the pig balanced, picked the grass off one side of it, and rolled the barbecue back into the street.

Mr. Jefferson offered to hose the bacon bits off the bouncer himself so we could get on our way.

We'd only walked a few steps down the road when Mom leaned out of the car. "I hope you boys brought your driver's licenses." And then we heard my parents laughing really hard.

"Your folks really know how to have a good time, don't they?" Toby let go of the greasy barbecue and walked a few feet behind me while I drove it.

8

If I ignored everything going on around me and didn't think about it too much, it was actually fun to be pushing the stupid thing down the middle of the street—a thought that creeped me out big time. When the museum was only about fifty feet away, I heard it: the clicking. At first I didn't know what it was, but then I saw a camera sticking out of a bush. I spotted a bicycle lying on the ground nearby.

Click. Click. Lizzie stepped out from behind the bushes. "Nice smile," she said, and pointed the camera at me again. *Click.* She hopped on her bike and sped off.

"Hey!" Toby yelled after her.

I had no idea why Lizzie was always doing stuff like that to me. "You've got to erase those photos, Toby."

"Don't worry," Toby said, and started after her. "I'll get that camera even if I have to do it in the middle of the night."

I was doomed with or without photos, because Lizzie'd blab this story all over anyway. There was one thing everybody knew about Lizzie: she was a blabber.

2

Dad's catering staff was waiting for us by the picnic benches in the museum's small park and garden. I said hello, then planted the barbecue under Dad's sign and walked away from it as fast as I could.

DEAD MEAT
Catering and Events
IF YOU CAN CATCH IT,
WE CAN COOK IT

Forty security guards and their families were there for the picnic. Because Mom was head of security, she was in charge of planning and supervising everything for the whole day.

Mom hurried to the gazebo on the grass and grabbed the microphone. "Let's get this party started," Mom's voice sang. "My husband, Bob, and his Dead Meat catering team are cooking pig for us. Art bingo will start in ten minutes, followed by the Picasso look-alike contest. And my son, Matisse . . ." She picked me out of the crowd and pointed; everyone turned to face me.

I knew everybody who was looking at me. After all, I've been going to the art museum to paint every day after school for five years. I copy the paintings on the walls.

Mom tilted her head to one side and a big smile took over her whole face. "I've arranged an outdoor exhibit of Matisse's copies of the masterpieces we have here at our museum. He hasn't come near copying all three hundred and fifty paintings in Geraldine Emmett's collection of nineteenth- and twentieth-century art, but he's giving it a try." Mom has a lot of wishes and hopes about art and me, like she had about Frida, but then Frida got stuck on purple. Mom wants at least one of us kids to be an artist. I guess if I don't work out, she'll have one more shot with Man Ray.

I want to have my own paintings hanging in the museum one day. I like to paint, but so far I only copy other people's paintings. I'm working my way up to painting something using my own ideas, but hanging around the museum sure makes it seem like every idea has been used up and done perfectly by somebody else already.

Mom redirected attention away from me and onto the smoke wafting from Dad's barbecue.

I walked around and ended up under the trees next to the picnic area. On the ground were lots of acorns in odd shapes and sizes. I picked some up and put them in my pockets. There were clumps of bright red berries too. For fun, I squished the berries with a rock and spread the red pulpy stuff on a patch of dirt, then shaped it to look like the flames of a fire. I crumpled some dry leaves and dropped them so that they made the letters SOS above the berry-pulp fire. With a stick, I drew a pig running away from the fire. Then I drew myself riding the pig, holding a white surrender flag made out of a gum wrapper. I used four acorns for eyes and saved the rest to take home. I stepped back to look at what I'd created.

Mr. Kramer, one of the guards who worked for Mom, walked up to me. "Hey, Matisse." He couldn't have been looking where his feet were going because he stepped right on my artwork in the dirt.

"Mr. Kramer, you're . . ." I pointed at his foot on the SOS, but I guess he didn't hear me, because he kept shifting his weight from foot to foot and shuffling around.

"Matisse, I just wanted to let you know how much I like your copies." His foot moved on top of me riding the pig. "Your paintings look as good as the real ones."

"Thank you."

"But I was just wondering, do you ever do other artwork?" Mr. Kramer asked.

"What do you mean?"

"Do you ever create anything inspired by your own life?"

"Well . . ." I looked down at the ground, and then over at my family. Mom had her mouth on the helium-tank hose, Dad was hopping on one foot, Frida was ripping a purple flower up by its roots, and Man Ray had just eaten something he'd pulled out of his ear.

"Never."

3

The cooking smells the next morning confirmed what I'd already feared. There'd be leftover-piggy surprises all week.

Dad had his nose over a frying pan, sniffing as he stirred the food with a wooden spoon. His sprained ankle looked as if it' had had a run-in with maroon and lime green chalk and a bike pump. It was hard to believe he could stand on it.

Man Ray had a toy stethoscope around his neck. He was sitting on the floor near Dad, trying to listen to Dad's bad ankle. "Daddy, ouwie," he said. Every Band-Aid we owned was on the floor.

"Man Ray is my doctor." Dad patted him on the head.

Mom, dressed for duty, was at the kitchen table. She wears all-black clothes and special no-noise shoes—like nurses' shoes, except they're black, so they match up nicely with her security clothes. Her coffee had kicked in, and she was filling in the little squares in speedy motion on a three-by-three-foot work calendar. "Matisse is finally here!" she said, and looked back down at her work.

Mom didn't mean me, though. She meant the big important artist Henri Matisse. An exhibition of his work was opening at our museum.

"Matisse, I hope you're hungry," Dad said.

"I'm always hungry." Sometimes all I wanted was a PB&J, but that didn't fit in with the extreme eating that went on at our house.

"That's the only reason to have kids—they're born hungry and they stay that way," Dad said.

Mom and Dad both laughed really hard in that weird way of theirs.

Frida flew into the room and dropped her math homework and a pencil in front of me. "Hi. Numbers four, ten, and twelve. Please."

Frida gave me her geometry word problems all the time, and I drew angles and shapes so she could see what her teachers were asking her. I liked helping her. But she and her friends had given each other

15

makeovers last night, and looking at what she did to herself made me mad. "I'm not helping you until you wash the purple dye out of your hair."

"It'll take three months to wear off."

"Why can't you look like everybody else?"

"Haven't you heard, Matisse? Being like everybody else is overrated," Frida said. "I'm being myself. Who are you?"

"Enough," Dad said as he hop-stepped a couple of plates full of food to the table. "Concentrate on your food."

"I don't think I can eat with her hair in the same room."

"Stop," Mom snapped. "Frida, I like the purple better than your usual brown." She rolled up her calendar and put a rubber band around it. "Matisse, put this by the door. Frida, help Man Ray into his high chair."

Mom and Dad acted like they didn't even care that Frida's hair was the color of a Skittle. They're lucky I'd never do anything like that.

It was quiet for a few minutes while we ate Dad's breakfast creation. We are the tasting committee for his business and his new book, *The Dead Meat Maestro*.

"I'm experimenting with the pork leftovers. Yummy for crummy?" he asked.

"Really yummy, honey." Mom smiled, then looked at her watch.

"No. No. No," Man Ray said.

It tasted like chicken but with a funny flavor, as if the pig had spoken Spanish or something. The drippy sauce had me worried. "Did you put this in my lunch?" I asked.

"Absolutely."

Sauce has seeped out of my backpack a few times at school. It's scary how fast a million-man ant march can get up and going in the back of the classroom. And it's scary how long kids remember it.

Frida's taste buds are the same as those of Dad's clientele. So he wants her opinion the most. After getting our attention, she rolled the food around in her mouth for effect. "Umm—hmm." *Gulp.* "It's got a savory taste, but it's leaving a filmy feeling on the roof of my mouth. It's kind of . . . slimy." She put her fork down. "Sorry, Daddy."

Dad is known for his lumberjack food: rugged, crispy, crunchy—never slimy. He believes in batter, BBQ sauce, salt, and big portions. "Back to the butcher," he said.

Mom pushed her chair out with the back of her legs and took her plate to the sink. "Sorry to rush, but there's a logistical nightmare brewing at the museum. The security system overhaul starts tonight, and I've got twenty-six school visits to organize." She looked at me with her isn't-it-exciting face. "And the Henri Matisse show opens. Yeah." She grabbed her things, gave Dad a kiss, and picked up Man Ray. "I'm heading to the car."

"Matisse, Frida, don't keep your mom waiting," Dad said. "Dishes in the sink, and take your lunch on the way out."

Mom stopped at Never-Never Land Day Care first, and took Man Ray inside. Before we got to my school, I stuck my liquidy lunch on the floor of the backseat and put a road map and a box of tissues on top of it. I'd get Toby to share his food with me. I hoped it wouldn't be pork and beans.

4

Toby had accidentally fallen asleep when he should have been deleting the images of me in Lizzie's camera. So, before class, I needed to hunt down the photos she had printed and plastered all over school.

The picture was evidence that I had pushed Dad's barbecue, but the worst part about it was the pig-eating smile on my face.

I met Toby at the end of the hall. We had found nineteen copies. "Nobody prints nineteen of anything," I said.

"Yeah," Toby said. "There must be one someplace

else to make twenty, or six to make twenty-five, or . . ."

"We checked everywhere, right?"

"Not the girls' bathroom. There could be one there, or six, or—"

"Okay, okay." I ripped the nineteen photos into tiny pieces and hid them in my backpack. "Your sister is a brat."

"This is nothing. Try having almost the same face or sharing every toy you've ever gotten since the day you were born."

"Why does she have to torture me?"

"You know why."

When I was six and a half, I wrote Lizzie a poem asking her to marry me. She said yes. When I was nine, I unasked her.

"Can't a person make one mistake?"

"Girls never get over their first love," Toby said.

"That's horrible, and it better not be true."

We walked down the hall and into our classroom. Ms. Knuckles was writing questions on the whiteboard and kids were pulling out their notebooks. It seemed like any other Monday morning. Then Lizzie made her grand entrance.

"Number twenty just walked in the room," Toby said from two rows over.

Lizzie strutted in front of the class with her shoulders back and her hands on her hips like she was

Superwoman or somebody. The twentieth photo was paper-clipped to the front of her T-shirt. She must hate me more than any person she's ever met in her entire life. My dodo grin was right in the middle of Lizzie's chest.

The class cracked up when they saw it.

And that was the moment I became a member of my own family.

Ms. Knuckles turned around from the board. "Quiet, please. Lizzie, sit down."

On the way to her desk, Lizzie gave me a wave and a smile like I would be happy to see her.

It would be fine with me if she vaporized on the spot.

Ms. Knuckles got a yardstick and poked it in the center of the U.S. map pinned to the wall, then she tapped the first question on the whiteboard. "What is the largest state?"

I slumped down in my seat and half heard the other questions Ms. Knuckles read off the board. "Do states surrounding the Colorado River share water?" "Where are the different time zones?"

While Ms. Knuckles talked, kids sent notes to each other about Lizzie's T-shirt. I was busy thinking of reasons to convince Ms. Knuckles I needed to be homeschooled.

The recess bell finally rang and everyone took off down the hall. But Ms. Knuckles asked me to stay after class.

"Matisse," she said. "I know you copy artwork at the museum. And you like that, right?"

"Um, yeah." I tried to sound sick, so she'd let me go home if I asked.

"Well," Ms. Knuckles said, "the copier is broken, and the computer printer I share is backed up for hours. Could you draw fourteen copies of this map? Only half the class got copies." She held up a line drawing of the United States without the names of the states. "You could trace it, or whatever it is you do, so we—"

I didn't wait for her to finish. "I'll do it," I said. "But I can't work here. I have to go someplace else."

"Pack up your things." Ms. Knuckles unlocked the door behind her desk. The door opened onto a room that she shared with three other teachers for meetings and extra supplies. She shoved a plastic volcano and boxes of paper clips and chalk to one side of the table. She slapped a stack of paper in front of me and dug around for the tub of assorted color pencils and pens. "Take your time. This is so nice of you." She smiled at me and left the room.

It was easy to copy the map. I made a few copies by tracing it, then did some freehand. I hid the original before drawing a couple from memory. It didn't take me long to do all the copies, but there was no way I was going to go back to class so soon. Filling in the states with different colors on a few of the maps helped me kill a lot of time. Then I made an extra copy, real slow. After tracing and coloring, I cut the states out with scissors. There were more than fifty pieces of colored paper on the table, counting the islands of Hawaii and Alaska. The pieces looked good arranged in lots of ways, but I picked one way and glued them back onto a new sheet of paper. It was from smallest to largest, in a spiral pattern like you see on the side of a snail or in pictures of galaxies. I blew on the wet glue.

Ms. Knuckles stuck her head in the door. "Finished yet? You've already missed math."

"All done." I dropped the spiral map down to my side. She would be mad that I used school supplies for it.

"Thank you so much." She flipped through the maps. "These are . . . colorful. What's in your hand?"

"It's nothing."

"Let me see." Ms. Knuckles took my spiral map from me. "Wow, Matisse. Look at this thing." She turned it around and around.

"I used your stuff. Sorry."

"You're so creative. This is so . . . you." She handed the map back to me.

"It's not me. I was just fooling around."

"Back to class," Ms. Knuckles said, killing my plan to stay in the office until lunch.

"Look at these supercolorful maps Matisse

made," she said to the class when we walked into the room. She held them up. "Show them the other one you made, Matisse."

"It's an extra one," I said.

"It's beautiful. Hold it up."

I held up the map that was supposed to be only for me.

The class was quiet.

"In a galaxy far, far away," someone said.

Then came the *Twilight Zone* song: "Do do do do do do do do."

"That's a crazy person's map!" someone shouted. Everybody laughed.

"That's enough," Ms. Knuckles said.

"That should go up—" Lizzie started.

"In a museum." Toby cut in, trying to stop whatever she was up to. "That's what Matisse wants."

I stared hard at Toby.

"Can I put it up in the display case next to Jenny's pipe cleaner atom?" Lizzie asked. She runs the school decorating committee.

"No." I didn't want the map up anywhere. I was just goofing around, killing time.

Ring! The lunch bell went off.

I waited until everyone was gone except Toby. "It's supposed to be a secret that I want my art up in a museum!"

"Sorry. I thought the map was cool. Everybody already knows you're more artistic than the rest of us."

Toby was mostly right. I was artistic, but not necessarily in a good way. "I'm so far away from— I should give it up."

"Don't give it up, but you *could* go to the park with me after school sometimes and play ball instead of going to the museum."

"I don't like games with balls, and I'm not good at them either."

"That doesn't stop the rest of us from playing," Toby said.

5

After school I took a detour past the park. I didn't see Toby, but it did look like it might be fun to hang out there sometimes. I would have to tell Mom that I was giving up the museum to go to the park with Toby, and that I needed cleats, a glove, or a stick.

A huge banner with Henri Matisse's signature was hanging above the museum doors. Lots of loyal art fans were there because it was opening day of the new exhibition.

Mr. Carter was guarding the front entrance. "Slap me five," he said when I got to the top of the steps. "Your mom's waiting for you."

"Hey." I high-fived him and went inside. People were waiting in line to buy tickets. I stepped around to the other side of the ticket counter to get my identification badge. As I leaned over the edge of the counter I saw a bluish-white hairy thing. It was Prudence, the oldest person to volunteer for anything, squatting down near the floor. If she's not helping someone with tickets or directions, we're helping her.

"Darn it," Prudence said. "My knees are stuck."

I went around the desk and grabbed Prudence by her elbows and lifted her up. Her knees popped.

"Can you hand me those Henri Matisse brochures?" she asked. "We're going through them like mad today."

I did, then took my badge from the top drawer.

"Matisse, help me sit down." Prudence reached out and gripped my hands.

I braced the side of my foot in front of her sturdy lace-ups and lowered her in slow motion into the chair like I was docking with the space station.

"Have you seen your mother?" she asked.

"Not yet."

"You're to drop your things in the office and hurry to the east gallery. Your homework can wait." Prudence shooed me along.

Mom's office is to the side of the front desk. The door has SECURITY PERSONNEL ONLY printed on it, but I get to go in anyway. It's the nerve center of the place. Staff members stop here before taking their things to the guards' locker room at the back of the museum. They check here for updates posted on a long wall covered with lists and calendars.

"Hi there," Ms. Whitsit said when I walked in. She was setting Security Master Plan notebooks on the conference table in the middle of the room. Laminated grids of the floor plan, air ducts, and wiring were propped up at the end of the table. "We couldn't be busier if we were the United Nations. Are you excited about the Henri Matisse show?"

"I think so."

Mom's desk is in the far corner after you pass the see-through glass wall that looks into the Operations Room. That room is always locked, and you need a special key to get in there. I knocked on the glass.

Three guards inside the room turned around from the bank of video images and the alarm switchboard. They waved to me.

I dropped my backpack under Mom's desk.

Since Toby had only been able to share an apple and some Fig Newtons, I was starving. I headed across the main corridor to the gift shop. Today they had tiny chocolate bars with paintings by Picasso printed on the wrappers. I held four of them up for Mr. Mulligan to see.

Mr. Mulligan was behind the cash register, helping

a customer. He waved me on and said, "I'll put it on your tab."

I took the first right down the main hall. It was busier than usual, and everybody I passed had a Matisse brochure in his or her hands. Mom was at the far end of the corridor.

When she spotted me, she flung her arms high in the air and kept them up until she reached me. "Matisse. Oh boy!" she said. She grabbed my arms and positioned my body in the direction of the east gallery and we started walking. "Matisse. Wait until you see— Oh boy!"

I figured I'd wait until I'd looked at the new exhibition before I told Mom I was going to be playing ball at the park.

"Close your eyes," she said.

"What for?"

"For fun. I'll guide you. Close your eyes." She put her hands on my shoulders.

We moved faster than I wanted to with my eyes closed. We were dodging in and out among the people and the rubber soles on my shoes made loud screeches on the marble floor. When we got to the Matisse room I could feel more people around us, and our steps got smaller and smaller until finally we stopped, and she let me go.

"You can open your eyes now."

A painting by Henri Matisse was right in front of

me. A bright arrangement of colors filled my view. We'd never had a real Henri Matisse painting at our museum. The room was full of colorful paintings. Stuff I recognized from the posters all over my bedroom, the art books on our coffee table, and the coloring books I'd filled in when I was little. The guy everybody talks to me about: Him. Me. Matisse.

Mom was having a moment with a painting right next to me. She never just looks at a painting. She puts her nose a foot away and slowly starts stepping backward, keeping her eyes in the center of the painting. Then all of a sudden she'll stop, stay in that position until, out of the blue—and you never know how long it will be—she'll say, "What an experience." And she's done.

Mom was in a trance looking at a painting. "Matisse," she said softly. "Oh, Matisse." She clasped her hands together in prayer and aimed her dreamy look at me. "These paintings are on loan from the collection of Henri Matisse's own son Pierre. And Pierre's private collection is spectacular. Henri Matisse was the man I was thinking of when you were born."

"That's so icky, Mom."

"Besides your father, of course." She clenched my shoulders in her hands and we started to walk again, stopping at every painting. Our final destination in the room was my portable easel, which she had already set up off to the side with my paints and brushes. There was a blank canvas set in position. "I'm very excited," Mom said.

I looked around the room.

"Do you want to paint?" Mom asked.

Mom didn't know I had plans to go to the park starting soon. But looking at Henri Matisse's paintings made me want to stay at the museum. It was going to be hard living up to my namesake. His paintings were simple and complicated, both at the same time. Luckily, most of his work looked like a kid had painted it anyway. And besides, I'd been practicing for this my whole life.

Mom looked at her watch. "I've got a meeting. Last one before the alarm system overhaul starts tonight." She beamed at me. "So . . . you want to paint?"

There was only one answer Mom wanted to hear. I grabbed a paintbrush. "I'm ready."

6

I put my park plan on pause, and for the next two weeks I painted Matisses at the museum. I'd get my homework done first in Mom's office, and then I'd go paint. By the time I got started every day there were only two hours left before closing. The museum was less crowded then, and I didn't get in anyone's way. Each night mom and I would greet the security alarm installers when we left. They worked on the new system during the night so that the museum could stay open during the day.

Mom blew in and out of the Matisse room every afternoon, and she'd bang on my arm and say, "These are the best copies you've ever done. I named you right, didn't I? Huh?" She took all my paintings home and hung them in the minigallery she had set up at the house.

Working clockwise around the room, I copied Henri Matisse's pictures, one by one.

I was copying *Portrait of Pierre Matisse*. It's a picture of Matisse's son, Pierre, as a kid. It's an oil sketch more than a painting, and it wasn't even framed with glass in front of it.

And except for the stupid pink thing on his head—which I would never wear—Pierre kind of looked like me. Our hair color was the same, we both had solid black marbles for eyes, and he could have been in sixth grade just like me.

I copied *Portrait of Pierre*, but it didn't come out right, so I added glasses and a mustache to it for fun. I tried it again on a new canvas, but it still wasn't right, so it didn't matter when I gave him buckteeth and a patch over one eye.

My next *Portrait of Pierre* turned out great. Because of the practice I got from the first two copies, the third one was easy. The picture practically painted itself. Everything looked good: the colors, the thickness of the paint, the direction of the brushstrokes, and the look on Pierre's face.

Mr. Snailby, the guard posted in the Matisse room, noticed. "It's perfect."

Mr. Snailby and I were admiring my *Portrait of Pierre* when Mom flew into the gallery.

She pulled Mr. Snailby and me into a huddle. She was talking fast and her face was all twisted up. "The new security system is malfunctioning. They worked on the west gallery last night, but it wasn't patched in properly and the whole thing has shorted out. Every light on the console is off. No video—nothing. The paintings are not protected. Code red," she said. "Anyone could walk in here and take a painting right off the wall—and we wouldn't even know it." Mom wasn't breathing. Her eyes darted around the room like she was an undercover spy. "Mr. Snailby, you know the grid better than anybody. You have to come with me. Matisse, stay here. You are in charge of this room." She pointed all her fingers at me like she was casting a spell, and then she did the same thing in the direction of all the Matisse paintings on the walls. "These are your responsibility."

She dashed around the room telling people the museum was closing early, and she ushered them out the door, along with Mr. Snailby.

I was alone. I'd never been there without a guard nearby or visitors roaming around.

The little red lights under the surveillance cameras in both corners of the room were off. I was really alone. No one could see me.

I knew I shouldn't do it. It was wrong. But I

34

stepped over the tape line on the floor in front of *Portrait of Pierre*. That's normally when a security guard would say, "Too close, step back." To be a whole foot inside the tape line made it more interesting to look at the painting. When else would I have a chance like this? I was so close to it, I could feel the colors rushing through me, or maybe it was something else, because a strange noise came out of my throat.

The motion-detection beams that usually shone down from the ceiling were off too.

Then I did a really bad thing. I reached up . . . and touched the frame. If the motion alarm had been working, it would have gone off, and probably someone would have tackled me to the ground.

I thought of doing something else bad. It was so bad and wrong it was stupid. I felt sick just thinking it. But that didn't stop me. I grabbed the frame around *Portrait of Pierre* and took the whole thing off the wall. As I stood with the painting in my hands, a whole bunch of new noises came out of me, and it felt like a heat lamp was melting the skin on the back of my neck.

What I did next was really stupid—but mostly illegal. I turned the frame around. The canvas was held in place by some sort of little nails stuck into the frame on all four sides. I was surprised they were so easy to get out. I was operating as if someone else were controlling me. How could I be doing that? It was unbelievable when I lifted the masterpiece right out of the frame. I leaned it against the wall. I took my fake *Portrait of Pierre* and stuck it in the frame. I jammed a couple of the nails back in to hold it for a minute while I took a quick look, dropping the other nails into my pocket to keep them together.

I hung the frame back on the wall with my painting in it.

There I was, looking at something I had painted hanging in an art museum. I wasn't getting enough air, and I had a tingling feeling all over my face, but it was worth it.

It looked really, really good.

What other kid in class could do that?

Nobody. That's who.

7

I heard footsteps coming down the corridor. I lunged at the painting, but before I could do anything, a tour group led by Prudence came into the room.

"Ahhh!" one of the people on the tour gasped.

I slapped my hands down and gripped my jeans in my fists. I didn't turn around. The masterpiece was sitting on the floor. I could feel the tour group coming up behind me.

Prudence turned me around and put her face an inch from my name tag. "Who's this?"

"It's me, Matisse."

"Hello, talented boy," she said.

As the group gathered around, I lifted the ancient painting off the floor with the fewest fingers I could use without dropping it. Placing it on my easel, I sat down on my stool.

Prudence stuck her face close to the placard on the wall and read aloud: "Portrait of Pierre Matisse, by Henri Matisse." Then she stepped back and began her lecture. "This is a portrait of Matisse's son Pierre. Matisse used the image of his son Pierre in only two other paintings."

Everyone focused on my painting on the wall. I was seconds away from the art lovers' figuring out what I had done and pinning me in a hammerlock.

"And I'm pleased to tell you that Pierre is an old geezer still barking at the moon at only eighty-nine years young."

The group tittered along with Prudence.

I wondered if they would still be amused when my phony art fell out of the frame and hit someone in the shin.

They pointed at my fake and smiled. They tilted their heads and squinted, while sweat gathered on my upper lip.

"It seems even lovelier than it was when I saw it yesterday," Prudence said. "The colors and the emotion come together in a beautiful expression of the artist's love for his son. Come in closer and observe the quality of the brushstrokes."

Everybody studied my copy even harder. My forehead turned into a waterfall. What was going on? As far as I could tell, they liked my painting as much as they would have liked the real one.

It didn't look like anyone was noticing that a kid did the painting they were looking at. How was that possible? I dried my face on my shirtsleeve and I began to cool off a little bit. It was actually pretty neat, watching people admire my work. I had completely fooled them. I leaned back, stretched out my legs, and put my hands behind my head.

Every muscle in my face was smiling, not to mention every tooth in my head making an appearance, when a woman on the tour pointed at me. "That boy," she said. "He's wearing the same shirt as the boy in the painting."

What was she talking about? I shot my eyes down at my shirt. Jeez, she was right: I was wearing a striped shirt just like the one Pierre had on in the painting. Ick! When I looked up, all their faces were turned toward me. My lips slammed together and I began sweating all over again.

"This is Matisse," Prudence said. "Isn't that a coincidence? This Matisse's work will be up in a museum one day too." She smiled at me. "Don't you think so, Matisse?"

I pulled my arms in and faked a cough into my fist. "It's funny you should say that."

Prudence leaned in over my head to see what was on my easel. I was folded in half when she finally focused her eyes. "Oh my, that's nice," she said. "Gather around this talented boy," she told the group. "He copies the paintings we have here at the museum. Let's watch him work."

The people in the tour bunched in tight behind my easel, which held the real Matisse.

"Show us how you paint," Prudence prodded.

In a flash, I saw myself hog-tied to the bumper of a patrol car. "Gee. Maybe another time. This one's done." I tried to sound calm.

"There must be something you could add to it." Prudence looked at my fake in the frame. "Try to make it as nice as the one on the wall."

Aaahhh! What was the matter with her? This was a masterpiece!

"Don't make me beg in front of all these people, Matisse."

Now I was getting mad. I didn't want to upset Prudence or make a scene, so I squished out some paint onto my palette. Then I mixed a few colors in slow motion. I thought they would've gotten bored and moved on, but they stayed, breathing down my neck. When my palette was full, I fiddled with my brushes, and when I absolutely had to, I loaded one with paint.

Prudence was wheezing into my hair.

I slowly brought the brush up to the zillion-dollar painting. My hand was moist and shaky. I froze with the brush hanging in the air two inches away from the real *Portrait of Pierre.*

They waited.

"Go on," Prudence said. "Don't be shy." For encouragement, she banged my arm that was holding the brush toward the painting. Sweet old Prudence almost made me blob paint on Pierre's eyebrow!

"What's this? What's this?" Mom walked into the room.

I was never so happy to see her.

"Prudence! Didn't you see the signs? We're closing early today." Mom pointed to the exit sign. "Sorry, everybody. You have to go."

They all moaned and backed away from my easel and headed for the exit.

As Mom got closer to me, I didn't know which painting to throw my body in front of, my fake on the wall or the real one on my easel.

"That was a close one," Mom said. "The alarm hasn't been fixed yet."

Mom will see that it's not the real painting on the wall, I thought. She has eyes to the tenth power. She notices if one book is in a different place on the shelf at home. She'll just feel it. "Something's different here," she'll say. And she's always right. I just hope she will understand why I wanted to try it.

Mom started to leave, but she stopped, pivoted, and walked back. She was having a moment with my painting in the frame on the wall. Her eyes were telling her everything. She put her hands on her hips and looked harder. She was sniffing the air. She looked at me; I dropped my head. Mom took her time getting the words out. "What's different about this painting, Matisse?"

"Well, it's . . ." I wasn't sure what to say.

"C'mon, tell me if you notice anything about this painting."

"Mom, I just . . ."

"Tell me if you see it, Matisse."

Mom was not pleased. I thought she would understand why I would want to see something I painted hanging on the wall of a museum. Isn't this what she dreamed about for me? Maybe not exactly like this, but— "I'm really sorry, Mom."

She spun her head around to all the paintings in the room. "I can't believe you don't see it. This is the only painting that doesn't have a signature. It's not signed."

I blinked. Had she not caught on?

She raised her eyebrows. "Sometimes they signed them on the back. Let's just take a peek." She reached her hands up to the fake on the wall and her fingertips were almost touching the frame when she stopped. "What am I doing?" She put her hands up in the air like she was being arrested. "I'm acting as if it would be okay for me to touch the frame just because there is no alarm. Ha. Jeez. That would get me fired for sure." She made one last stop at my easel and looked at the masterpiece. "Wow."

"Yeah," I said.

"That's fabulous." She looked at me. "The matching shirt thing is cute. So what's the lesson here, Matisse?"

"Mom . . . I'm really not sure."

"There is a lesson here."

"What?"

"Make sure you sign your paintings."

"Oookaaaay."

"I need to find out if they've fixed the problem yet," she said, and hurried off.

Was my copy actually good enough to fool Mom? As soon as she was out of sight, I grabbed the frame, but it was too late. The motion-detection lights were back on. A blaring alarm went off.

Then I heard the approaching cattle drive charging down the hall. The museum SWAT team stormed the room. I was facing the wall. I froze.

"Put your hands in the air and step to the center of the room," one of the security officers said to me.

I turned around.

Four officers were in the room; their hands were resting on their batons.

My bladder banged around inside my body. My knees slammed together. "It's just me."

"Matisse?" Mr. Kramer said. "What are you still doing in here? We're closed. No one is supposed to be in the museum."

"I . . . I . . ."

"Matisse, we have a security problem in the museum right now and we can't have you fooling around in here. This is serious business," Mr. Kramer said. "You can put your hands down."

"Yes, sir."

Mom came back into the room.

"We were just about to arrest Matisse here," Mr. Kramer said.

"What?"

"Looks like a false alarm. The system isn't fixed yet."

"Apparently not," Mom said.

"We're going to need everyone out of the museum. The installers have to tear this place apart tonight. Everybody's got to be cleared out," Mr. Kramer said.

"My fault," Mom said. "I told Matisse to watch this room for me, and be the temporary guard while we were in code red."

"Sorry, Matisse." Mr. Kramer patted me on the back. "Appreciate your help, you're a good kid."

"Luckily, we are closed tomorrow," Mom said.

"But if they don't figure out the wiring, the musuem could be closed for days. The night crew is already here. It's going to be a long night for me. I'll take you home, Matisse, so I can get right back." She headed out with the other officers.

I needed to get the paintings switched back. But that didn't seem like a good idea with guards and big sticks just down the hall, not to mention how mad Mom would be. I'd have to wait until tomorrow, when the museum would be closed and the officers would be farther away. That was if someone didn't figure it out before then. The masterpiece looked so obvious just sitting there on my easel, but I didn't want to move it anywhere else. And right then I saw it: the masterpiece had no signature on it either. I tilted it forward. The painting was signed in red on the back. *J'adore Pierre. Papa Matisse.*

I closed the paint tubes and cleaned my brushes, then rolled my easel out of the way into the corner, just like always. Then I ran out the door.

I didn't sleep. In between instant replays in my head of the masterpiece switch, I wore the carpet out circling around, and I chewed my nails.

I couldn't turn on the light, since Man Ray was only six feet away from me in his big-boy bed, sleeping like a baby. He was lucky being only two years old; at that age you can make a mistake and be forgiven for it. But at eleven—you make a mistake, you pay. The grounding that would fit what I did was ginormous. There'd be a lot of trash cans to roll out front, and lawns to mow, and the number of TV shows I'd never watch would get into *Guinness*

World Records. I already wanted to cry from all the onions I'd have to chop for Chef de Dad.

Everything I said that morning at breakfast came out wrong. "Pass the sorry," I said.

Mom passed the salt.

"The meat tastes guilty."

No one noticed I was talking like a chucklehead.

"Breakfast tastes like a copy of one you made before, is that legal?"

Dad actually answered that question.

On the way to school, when Mom took Man Ray out of the car to drop him at day care, I said, "Have a nice fake."

I decided to shut up for the rest of the day, but Toby could tell something was wrong. "What's going on?" he asked, about a minute after he saw me.

"Nothing."

"Yeah. Right."

I spent the day worrying and not listening to my teachers. A police car siren went off outside during science class; the sound was coming from the direction of the museum, and that made me extra tense. I whacked my head on the corner of my desk ducking down when the principal, Mr. Baker, came into the room and whispered something to Ms. Knuckles.

Toby handed me his frozen juice box at lunch. "For the lump on your forehead," he said.

Best friends are annoying when you want to not be noticed.

"Something is going on, right?" Toby asked.

"You're right. But that's all I'm going to say."

"You should tell me, because you're going to explode."

I've never done anything Toby didn't know about. But maybe even he would think what I did was horrible. And Toby might spill the beans even if he didn't mean to. "When we are old guys in our twenties," I said, "I'll tell you about it over a couple of beers."

Near the end of the day, I had figured out a plan. It actually was the perfect day to switch the paintings back. On Tuesdays the museum gets cleaned. A big cleaning crew comes. They dust with germ-free rags and vacuum with sucker hoses that snake through the museum and shoot out exhaust into a special truck parked outside. The alarms inside are shut off so that the crew can work.

My last class was English.

"Write a short poem," Mr. Burnblum said. "You'll all read your poems aloud in small groups." When Mr. Burnblum assigned groups it meant he wanted school over as much as we did. He'd walk around and listen, and put a check by your name if you tried, but he'd never collect what we worked on.

My so-called poem was just a page full of words that rhymed with *stomachache*.

I got stuck with Steven, Brian, and Lizzie in my group.

"I'll go first." Steven, the guy we call "the Library," was the only person who took the assignment seriously. His poem was about being a perfect student.

Brian's poem was short. "How I like to eat. From hot, to sour, to sweet. The more I consume, the more I balloon. Everything's bigger but my feet."

Mr. Burnblum walked over to our group. "What have you got so far, Lizzie?"

Lizzie jumped. She didn't even have a piece of paper out. "Ummm." She fidgeted, then glared at me. "Ummm...Boys can be nice. Boys can be true. Ummm...But not the one I know. He belongs in a zoo."

Lizzie grinned and kept going.

"Roses are red. Violets are blue. Ummm...He's the most forgetful...est person I ever knew."

What a pest. I made up a poem on the spot too.

"What a killer memory. You didn't forget a thing. I suppose you dried the flower and kept the tinfoil ring. I was so over you before I was even eight. And now you're just annoying. And really, not that great."

School ended, and I was out the door.

* * *

The museum didn't look like it normally did. Scaffolding covered one side of the building. Workers in orange uniforms were up on platforms doing work on the windows. The vacuum truck was parked on the other side. Caution cones were blocking the front steps. Mrs. Rogers was at the top of the stairs, next to the front entrance. Normally only four guards came on cleaning day, and Mrs. Rogers wasn't one of them. She waved for me to come up.

I tried to act normal. "Hi, Mrs. Rogers. Isn't this your day off?"

"We're all doing overtime because of the renovation. You are the only one I am allowed to let inside." She turned to the door and unlocked it.

"Really. What's going on?"

"Everything you can think of, because of the code red yesterday. It's all listed on the bulletin board in the office."

Inside the museum was pandemonium. Lots of people I had never seen before were working. Extra tables were set up, and boxes of equipment were on the floor. I went into the office.

Mom was giving a talk to her staff. "Twice yesterday we had code-red situations. There's new equipment in every room, and there are alarm installers without security credentials inside the museum. Be alert for transgressions. Glitches and false alarms are bound to happen. Our goal is to keep the museum open, but as of now, the museum will be closed tomorrow, until partial or full security is ensured. Check for updates on the master calendar."

I put off the painting exchange one more day.

Trying to sleep was a joke. The next morning I got dressed early and ran to Toby's house. I couldn't keep it from him any longer. I threw a half-eaten Pop-Tart at his second-story window; a piece of it stuck to the screen.

Lizzie opened the window a crack. "What's up, dorkwad?"

"Where's Toby?" I asked.

"He's asleep."

"I need to talk to him."

"Where's the fire?"

"Tell him to go to the front door."

"Maybe." Lizzie pushed the window closed.

A few minutes later Toby came out his front door. "I'm not in my twenties yet, but go ahead, what's bugging you?"

"You may hate my guts when I tell you or think I'm the worst person you ever met."

"How bad could it be? Did you kill somebody?"

"It will kill my mom if she finds out." I couldn't even say it out loud. So I whispered it to him.

He stepped back. "That's definitely the stupidest thing you've ever done."

"And wrong."

"Just say, 'Oh, oops, everybody—I'm going to change these paintings back now'?"

"People at museums are very against oh-oops kinds of things. They are way sensitive about paintings."

"Museum people don't scare me. What do you want me to do?"

"Come with me to the museum after school. Tell your mom that you'll be with me this afternoon."

"You're supposed to be coming to the park with me to play baseball, not me going to the museum with you."

"Believe me, it's the last place I want to be too. But, Toby? There's a priceless masterpiece just sitting out in the open on my easel. I need your help."

***

After school Toby and I walked to the museum. He was bouncing a small rubber ball on the sidewalk while I told him the plan.

"You have to help me switch the paintings—if mine didn't already fall out. It has to be done really fast," I said.

"What if the alarm goes off?"

"The museum is closed today because the system shorted out. They'll think it's happened again. And they always let me inside. We'll be okay as long as we can get it done before anyone sees us do it."

"If we get caught, I don't want to have your mom say I can't come over to your house anymore."

"Don't worry."

When we got there, I had a lot to worry about. The museum was open.

"It was supposed to be closed!" I said. "This is bad."

Toby bounced his ball off my head. "Now what, Art Man?"

"I'm not sure. Follow me."

The museum was busy with people. Toby waited for me outside the Security Personnel Office. The video displays in the Operations Room were off. I knocked like normal to say hello, and the three guards inside were busy with wires and switches, but they looked up and waved to me. I checked the lists on the bulletin board before I left.

"Great news," I told Toby. "The cameras still aren't working." We hurried to the Matisse room; it was full of people. Mr. Snailby was in his usual position near the door.

Toby went up to the biggest painting in the room. "Is this it? That would be so cool if this was the one you painted."

"I copied this one, and the copy's already hanging in my dining room." I pushed Toby along until we got to *Portrait of Pierre*, which was about the size of a notebook.

"That's a small one. It's good, though," Toby said. "And I don't even like paintings." Toby banged me on the arm. "You know, it looks like a painting of you. If it had numbers under it, it could be your mug shot in a police lineup. Ha-ha."

A little girl and her mother came and stood next to us.

Toby pointed at my painting and spoke with a bad English accent. "Very, very fine and outstanding, don't you think?"

"Oh yes," the woman said.

I pinched the back of Toby's arm and pulled him away to the corner where my easel and the masterpiece should have been. But they weren't there. I rushed to Mr. Snailby. "Hi. Where is my painting stuff?"

"I stored it for you. The workers tore this place apart, and I took your things to a safe place."

"What safe place, Mr. Snailby?"

"The cleaning-supplies closet."

Toby and I wound our way through the corridors of the museum until we got to the closet. It was the size of a small bedroom. Bottles and mops and rags filled every shelf and corner. Jammed by the back wall was my easel. I grabbed it and turned it around, but *Portrait of Pierre* wasn't there.

"Toby, I don't see it!"

"So you're not the only one around here who does the wrong stuff with things that don't belong to them," Toby said.

Just then I saw it. It was right in front of us, lying faceup under a feather duster. I stared at it; I didn't touch it.

"Oh no!"

Toby looked at me, then at the painting, then back at me. "Is that bad?" Toby asked. "Why aren't you picking it up? It's bad, right?"

"There're books about how lousy dust is for art-work. You can major in it in college. This place is cleaner than a hospital because dust is full of mites and bunnies, and microscopic criminals, all little enemies of paintings."

"So we have to get it off, right." Toby lifted the duster off the painting. A thousand weensy flecks of poison fluttered down onto the painting. "I'll just brush that off," he said. He was about to rub his arm across the painting, but I grabbed his wrist.

"There are disgusting things on our skin that can stick to a painting. The nasty stuff decays and festers until the painting dies," I said.

"Eeeuuuooo," Toby said.

"I'll blow the dust off." I blew out a column of air. The dust leaned but didn't come off. "Okay, Toby, we need to do this together. When I say *three*, give it your best birthday-candle blow. Ready? One, two, threeee."

The dust came off in a cloud.

"Is spit as bad as skin and dust?" Toby pointed to the saliva droplets on the painting.

"Oh no! Probably, but . . . I hope not." I fanned the painting back and forth. Things were getting worse by the second. "We need to get it back to the gallery, but we've got to stop touching it."

I tried to put the painting under my T-shirt, but it wouldn't fit without coming into contact with my toxic skin. Toby had on a zippered sweatshirt. "We can put it between your T-shirt and your sweatshirt," I said.

"Sure. Hold this." Toby handed me the rubber ball and unzipped his sweatshirt. On his T-shirt was a streak of relish that had collided with something red and sticky.

"No way," I said.

Toby grabbed a paper towel roll and spun it around the painting like cotton candy. I didn't stop him. The acids in the paper towel could possibly hurt the painting, but I felt we could risk it for a short trip down the hall. Toby stuffed the priceless painting into his clothes, making a masterpiece-and-sweatshirt sandwich.

"Let's go," I said.

We were power-walking our way back to the Matisse room when I heard Mom say from behind us, in her loudest museum whisper, "Matisse. Toby."

"Don't turn around," I said to Toby. "Make this next left."

We rounded the corner fast and started running down the hall. Toby, who is not used to how marble floors grab the tips of your shoes whenever they feel like it, went airborne and took a flying header down the hall. The painting flew out from under his sweatshirt just before his chest hit the ground. Pierre slid across the floor, stopping in front of the elevator ten feet away.

For a few seconds, the world stopped. Then the elevator doors opened. Museumgoers emptied out into the hall. Two of them walked off to the right and one stopped to look at his watch. But one woman, who was reading a brochure, had no idea that she was about to put her foot through a million-dollar painting.

I threw the ball. It bounced once down the hall and hit the woman in the thigh just as she was going to step on the paper-toweled masterpiece.

"Ahhh!" she squealed, and moved back. She glared at us. "This is an art museum, not a racquetball court."

"Sorry," I said as I picked up the painting and the ball and kept going down the hall.

There were about twenty people in the Matisse room. Mr. Snailby was at the door. The little red light was off on both surveillance cameras.

"We have to wait until the room empties out," I said to Toby.

"What about him?" Toby pointed to Mr. Snailby.

"Don't worry," I said.

We zipped the masterpiece back into Toby's sweatshirt. We waited a long time until the museum was almost closed. It was dark out when the people were finally gone. I got close to a painting and looked up at the ceiling. I could see the motion-detection beams.

"You can back out if you want. And I wouldn't blame you if you did," I told Toby.

"I'm in."

"It's going to get really bad in here before it gets better," I warned him.

"I've come this far. Let's do it," Toby said.

"I'll be right back."

I walked up to Mr. Snailby and took a deep breath. I could see that his legs were hurting him by the way he was tilted a little forward. He was the oldest guy working at the museum. "It's been a long day," I said. "Why don't you go rest? I'll watch everything for you."

"I could really use the break. Thanks, Matisse," Mr. Snailby said.

I watched Mr. Snailby walk out the door to the bench down the hall. I spun around and marched back to Toby. I darted my eyes to one camera, then another—they were still off. "Now," I said.

Toby pulled out the bundled-up painting and started to unwrap it.

I grabbed the frame and lifted it off the wall. The alarm went off. It was so loud I couldn't think, and my fingers felt like ten overstuffed sausages. I could not wiggle the nails out of the back. It didn't take long before I heard people running down the hall. "Toby, stop. No time." I put my fake back on the wall.

Toby shoved the spiral of paper towels under his sweatshirt, and I took the painting out of his hands just as two security guards burst into the room. They were Mr. Kramer and Mr. Napoleonsky.

Toby and I looked as guilty as any two people could look.

Mr. Kramer used his key to open the alarm box. He flipped the OFF lever and turned toward us. "Who's on guard?"

Mr. Snailby hurried back into the room. "I am," he said.

"What's going on in here?" Mr. Kramer asked.

Mr. Snailby looked around the room at all the paintings, and shook his head. "Looks like a false alarm."

Mr. Kramer came over. "Matisse, every time you're around the alarm goes off."

"Let me check you boys out," Mr. Napoleonsky said.

Toby and I froze. I still had the painting in my hand.

Mr. Napoleonsky circled around us. "I don't see anything that might trip off the alarm." He lifted up my T-shirt. "No metal belt buckle." He frisked my pockets.

I reached my arms straight out from my sides. The painting was dangling in my hand.

"Nothing," he said. "How about you?" he said to Toby. "Do you have a walkie-talkie or steel-toed shoes that could be setting off the alarm?"

"No," Toby said.

Mr. Kramer tapped Toby's bulging sweatshirt full of paper towels. "What's this?"

"Oh, I was just . . . playing."

"Playing what?"

"I was playing . . ." Toby looked at me in a panic. "You know."

"I don't know," Mr. Kramer said.

"I was playing . . . pregnant." He pulled the wad of paper towels out of his shirt and sheepishly handed them to Mr. Kramer.

The guards started laughing just as Mom arrived.

"Not this room again," she said. "I had to leave my meeting when I saw the red lights flashing. There is a serious glitch in here."

"Dang if I can't figure out the snag," Mr. Kramer said.

"I told the higher-ups the motion detectors were fixed. My credibility is on the line if this doesn't get worked out soon." Mom looked worried.

She sighed, then looked at me. "Matisse, what have you got in your hands there?"

"Just, um . . . my painting."

She gripped the underside of the canvas with her fingers and pulled it toward her. My arms straightened out, but I didn't let go. "This one's ready to come home," she said.

I bugged my eyes out at Toby.

Toby grabbed another edge of the painting. "Matisse said I could have this one."

Toby made a great save, I thought. But all three of

us still had our hands on the painting, each one of us trying to win the game of painting-tug-of-war.

I let go. "Yeah, Mom. The painting is Toby's belated birthday present."

"I didn't know you liked art, Toby," Mom said.

"I don't."

"That's what I thought. You should get something you like for your birthday."

"Oh, I—I—maybe," Toby stammered. "I like art okay."

"Give me the painting. Matisse can buy you a gift you want."

"Oh . . . whatever." Toby released the painting. Mom had it.

"Good. I'll meet you boys at the car in fifteen minutes." Mom walked off with the masterpiece.

I could have run after her and told her everything— but the train had already left the station. It was taking off slow, but there was no stopping it. When Mom reached the doorway and turned into the hall, it was past the point of no return.

"Uh-oh." Toby realized what he'd done. "How did she do that?"

"Toby, when I get sent to juvenile hall, they won't need my mug shot, since the painting—exhibit A—is my mug shot."

"You know, technically, your mom is the one who is taking the painting out of the museum. She's the one who's going to need a mug shot—right after she loses her job."

"I don't want my mom to lose her job!"

"At least it will be safe at your house until you get it back here," Toby said.

"Does a black hole sound safe to you?"

16

The painting was in the trunk, and Mom drove like she usually did, which didn't include much braking. She hardly slowed up in front of Toby's house. He said goodbye to me like it would be the last time. "I hope you live through the night."

"Yeah, I hope so too."

"Good luck," Toby said.

Without thinking we gave each other a hug.

Mom was looking at us in her rearview mirror. "I feel like I'm watching a scene from a movie."

"Okay, bye."

"Hope to see more of you at the museum," Mom said.

"I doubt it" flew out of Toby's mouth. "Oh, sorry."

"I'm used to how you talk," Mom said.

Toby was barely out of the car before her foot hit the gas.

Mom drove up our hill, and the contents of the trunk shifted to the tail end of the car.

Our garage door was open. Dad was wearing rubber gloves and his lead apron. He was all aglow from the blowtorch flame and the molten metal on his worktable. Frida was also in the garage, behind a mountain of magazines.

Our garage is not typical. It's a combination barbecue factory–hobby headquarters–Santa's workshop, times one hundred, squared and doubled. It's an every-man-for-himself arts-and-crafts bonanza. The glue department alone has Stuck on You, Adhere Aplenty, Sticky Is Our Business, Strangle Hold, and Hold Till You Die, to name just a few. We each have our own work area.

Dad likes to drag his power tools and extension cords out onto the driveway. He melts and bangs metal into barbecues of distinction. People who like Dad's food want to get his unique equipment too. Besides barbecues, he creates customized smokers and brining tubs, and makes them right here in our driveway.

In Frida's area, there's a chair with purple velvet and gold trim that looks like it belonged to Louis XIV.

Her sewing machine hums during weekends and on school nights after homework. The purple thread loaded into it never changes. She's sewn a new outfit for herself every week since she was twelve. Her scary dressmaker's mannequin is shaped exactly like her, and it stares blankly off into space. We call it Fridakenstein. And piled near her are stacks of gossip and fashion magazines where she hunts for design ideas.

Dangling above where Mom sits is a mobile she made with her label maker. She printed out little-known art facts—that Michelangelo was only two inches taller than Toulouse-Lautrec, for example, and that Vermeer painted only thirty-four paintings in his whole career. Under the glass on her desk are postcards of her one hundred favorite paintings. Everything is neatly squared up, numbered, and alphabetized. And for security practice, museum-quality motion detectors and a video camera are pointed at her desk twenty-four hours a day.

My workstation is in the back of the garage, so I can't be seen too easily from the street. I have a table that was once a door, and behind it are shelves that are loaded up with things I've collected. I'm what you call a hunter-gatherer. The cardboard boxes and jars are labeled with the names of people or places. Some boxes are full of everyday stuff like tickets, report cards, and crumpled wrappers. Others have things from nature, or scraps from my old paintings, or clippings from magazines. I like to pick out things from my collections and put them together all different. They're my own made-up time capsules. No one is allowed to see them. Frida spies on me sometimes though, because she knows it annoys me, and she takes things of mine and uses them on her outfits.

Man Ray has a sandbox that is mounted on wheels. We roll it into or out of the garage depending on who is watching him. It's full of toys, and there's a pillow and blanket for naps.

Frida came over to the car with a magazine in her hands. "It says here that Elvis has been in frozen animation, and that he was frozen in a purple robe. Elvis is alive."

"If Elvis is alive he's going to be very old," Mom said. She opened the car door, marched up to Dad, and knocked a few times on his helmet. "Hi, baby."

Dad stopped his work and made a fiery heart in the air with the blowtorch.

Mom bopped him two more times on the helmet and headed for her workstation. She put on goggles and grabbed the engraving gun.

I thought of leaving the painting in the trunk. But what if our car was stolen or locusts swarmed? "Mom. There's something I need to get from the trunk."

Mom lobbed me the keys. "I know. I'm making a new placard for your painting right now. Everything on the walls is rotating tonight."

I was afraid of that. I opened the trunk. Things had shifted around. Luckily, Pierre was on top. He was looking right at me.

I lightly touched the edges of the canvas as I lifted Pierre out. He had to be warned. "Anything could happen in there. Don't fall off the wall, don't talk to my sister, and don't show off. You're not staying long, so don't get comfortable." I slammed the trunk closed.

Frida was standing nearby. "Did your painting answer you back?"

"No. It's in frozen animation."

"That's not funny," she said, and disappeared.

A few minutes later, Mom came inside the house carrying the new placard, which had PORTRAIT OF PIERRE MATISSE BY MATISSE JONES engraved in the plastic. She placed it on the wall above the couch in the den, where every painting starts its rotation at Mom's minigallery. She moved all the other paintings and placards. Then she took the picture of Pierre from me and put it on the wall.

"There," she said, and then had one of her viewing moments. "There is something about this one, isn't there?" She was drumming her fingertips on her hips. "Maybe I like it so much because you look like Pierre. Don't you think? That must be it. It's as if we're hanging a portrait of you." She kissed my head. "I'll be right back." She returned a few minutes later with an arm hooked in one of Dad's. "Look at this, Bob. Doesn't it look just like Matisse?"

Dad was covered with metal filings. He flipped up his helmet visor. "Your first self-portrait."

Now everybody was noticing how much I looked like Pierre, and it was making me jumpy. "It's not a self-portrait; it's a picture of a guy named Pierre."

"Well, it sure looks like a self-portrait."

"It's not."

* * *

Later, when everybody was in bed, I snuck downstairs and took Pierre up to Man Ray's and my bedroom so I could keep an eye on him for the night. I wasn't sure where to put him—or should I say *it*? Whatever—*him, it, the thing,* or *my big problem.* I didn't want to just leave *him* anywhere because Man Ray might wake up and roll a little truck across *the thing* or take a crayon to *it.* The only place *it* fit was in the closet, down on the floor with our shoes, and I didn't want *him* to smell like dirty feet in the morning, so I tucked *my big problem* in bed with me. I even gave *it* my pillow. We lay there together for a while, but I couldn't fall asleep. I've been known to drool out of the side of my mouth and I couldn't expect tonight to be any different, so I took *him* back downstairs and put *him* back on the wall. I decided to lie on the couch and watch *the thing* from there.

Mom woke up. She came down in her kimono and snuggled into the couch with me.

It was time to tell Mom the bad news. But I needed to work my way up to confessing. I didn't want a vein to pop out in Mom's neck or have her eyeballs do loop-de-loops. I had to make my confession more like a fairy tale; if I were good at rhyming, I'd have turned the bad news into a poem. I had to soften the blow, partly because I didn't know CPR, but mostly because I've seen Mom's skill with a soldering gun and she could seal me into my room for a really long time.

"Mom."

"Yes?"

"Have you or Dad ever done anything wrong?"

"Ha. Yeah, well." She was jerking her head around and her eyebrows went up in the air.

"I mean something that isn't *that* wrong at first, but gets really wrong. A big goof that turns into a crime, sort of, that everybody gets really mad about."

"A crime! No! Is there something you need to tell me?" Mom sounded shocked.

If I wasn't the first criminal in our family and my behavior was hereditary, I could say it was an unruly gene inside me that made me do it. It was a theory. "Mom, please. I want to know."

"Well, let me think. Ummm . . . I took a friend's Girl Scout pin once. I took it off her desk at school when she was in the bathroom and pinned it to my sweater. I just wanted to try it on. When she came back, she was hysterical. 'Who took my pin? Call the principal, call my mommy.' The teacher had to stop class and we all had to look for it."

Yes! Mom stole something. "What did you do?"

"I went up to my friend and recited the Girl Scout pledge: 'I will do my best to be honest. . . .' She didn't notice the pin on my sweater. There I was, ready for her to say, 'Hey, you have my pin.' But she didn't. I couldn't believe it."

I shot a look up at Pierre. Bingo. "Did you give it back to her?"

"I threw my chest out and said: 'Be prepared.' The pin was right under her nose and she still didn't see it." Mom looked at me for a moment. "So I just fixed it. I took the pin off and put it back on her desk— which was what I was going to do in the first place. And it was all over."

It was hereditary. The only trait we had in

common, accidental thievery. "Did she ever know it was you?"

"I told her later."

"Was she mad?"

"Yes, and so was her mother. 'How could you steal from my daughter?' And her mother told my mother and I was grounded. I felt like nobody trusted me for a while. It was terrible."

I couldn't believe my luck. "You shouldn't have taken the pin, but you did, and even though you were never going to keep it you got in trouble for stealing something you didn't plan to take in the first place, right?"

"You know, I shouldn't have told her at all. Some things work out better when you just fix them yourself."

I wanted to make sure I was hearing Mom, the jewelry snatcher, correctly. "So, you wish you didn't tell anyone?"

"Well, yes, I guess I do." Mom yawned and got up. "Sleeping under the painting of you tonight?"

"Mom, it's not . . . Yeah."

"I love that," she said, and went upstairs.

My nonconfession confession went pretty well. The painting was right under her nose and she didn't notice. I was going to do what she did when she was a kid. I'd just fix it. Except maybe I wouldn't tell her later.

With a stolen painting in the house, it was hard to sleep, so I spent a few hours in the garage. I constructed license plates out of cardboard and cut-up strips of black rubber.

ART THIEF
SCARED
GROUNDED
DEAD MEAT

11

The next day at school, Toby and I sat in our usual spot at lunch.

"I dreamt the security guards were in my bedroom shooting arrows at me." I threw my grilled antelope sandwich back into my lunch bag.

Toby wasn't eating either.

"Hey, Toby. Look, I'll tell them I forced you into it," I said.

"It's not that." Toby kept looking at Lizzie and her friends at another table.

"What do you mean?" I asked.

"Well," he hedged. "It's, uh . . ."

I looked over at Lizzie and saw her talking and pointing at me. I got a sickening feeling. "You *didn't* tell Lizzie, did you?"

Toby had a sorry look on his face. "It slipped out."

"Slipped out!"

"Lizzie was bugging me, saying this and that about you, and I said, well, if Matisse was so dumb, how could he have a painting hanging in the museum?"

"She's going to blab it all over!"

Lizzie, Courtney, and Rose got up from their table and walked in our direction.

"Okay," Toby said. "Stay calm."

Lizzie was aiming another one of her mystery smiles at me. "Is it true?" she asked.

"What?" I said.

"You know."

"Not really."

"Do you have a painting hanging in the art museum?" Lizzie asked.

Something in the way Lizzie asked me made me want to say yes—like she would be impressed; like I would take a giant leap up in the respect department. But I knew it was just a trap. "Yeah," I said. "Haven't you heard? I'm the president of the solar system. Yoda is my uncle, and I'm going to sing the national anthem at the World Series. And, oh yeah, I have a painting in a museum." I reopened my lunch bag for effect. "Excuse me, we're trying to eat."

"Exactly," Toby said. "Matisse couldn't do that in a million years."

Lizzie looked back and forth between Toby and me. She locked eyes with me in that way that she does, and finally she said, "You can sing?"

"Get a grip." My sandwich tasted better than I thought it would.

The girls were about to leave, but Toby started talking. "Hey, big blabber. Matisse doesn't even . . ."

I slammed my knee into Toby under the table. "That's right," I said. "I don't even . . . like paintings . . . or the museum, there's no talking, don't touch, blah, blah, blah . . . What time at the park, Tobster? I'm with the national ball association now . . . the NBA. Right?" That didn't sound right at all. I nudged Toby.

"Yeah, Matisse goes to the park with me."

Lizzie and her friends turned to go.

"Find something else to talk about, blabber," Toby said.

"I wouldn't point fingers, blabbing runs in our family." Lizzie walked away.

"She's right, Toby."

"Really?" Toby turned his mouth into a zipper and zipped it shut.

"If you want me to keep going to school here, don't tell anyone else," I said.

He talked out of the corner of his mouth: "Glad you're coming to the park."

12

"You need this," Toby said. "A friendly game of baseball. What could you possibly miss in one day at the museum?"

"I hope you're right. Because avoiding my big problem is making me very tense."

"Try to forget about it."

A bunch of guys from our class met up on the baseball diamond at the park.

"Good, ten of us, it's even." Cooper's neck was thick, and his head was little. He was hammering a ball into his mitt. "Matisse, what position do you play? Artfield?"

"Very funny," I said. "First base." I figured a lower number would be easier than second or third. Then I added, "I can run."

"I just can't picture it. Ha-ha," Cooper laughed.

"I'll take Matisse on my team," Toby said.

"Fine." Cooper went to the pitcher's mound and started throwing balls to Kevin. Three other guys got gloves and took the field.

Toby, Jason, Brian, and I stood behind the backstop. Sam grabbed a bat.

"We hardly even keep score," Toby said. "There's no pressure. It's all for fun."

"Fun. Can't wait."

"I'm warmed up," Cooper said from the mound.

Sam stepped into the box and pulled his bat back. The first pitch was a ball.

"Good eye," Toby, Jason, and Brian shouted from behind the backstop.

Cooper's second pitch was a ball too.

"Make him work for it," Jason screamed while shaking the chain-link fence behind home.

"A walk is as good as a hit," Brian yelled.

Cooper threw a strike right down the middle. Sam didn't swing at it.

"Caught you playing statue, weenie," Cooper said.

"This one's coming right at you, butthead." Sam pointed at him. "Be ready."

"You be ready for my heat," Cooper answered.

"These guys aren't friendly," I said to Toby.

"A little competition never hurt anybody," Toby said.

"Eat this." Cooper fired one in.

Sam got a base hit. "Thanks for the snack, Cooper."

"Wait until you see what's for dinner, punk."

"I'm starting to feel a little pressure, Toby," I said.

"It makes you play better," Toby assured me.

Brian was second at bat. He took a couple of practice swings and accidentally hit the backstop twice. The guy can trip standing still. Brian hit the first pitch a long way, but he barely made it to first base.

Sam, who was on first base, made it all the way home. "Get a piece of my smoke!" he baited Cooper. "That's one to zero, babies."

"They're definitely keeping score," I said.

Toby grabbed my shoulder. "Listen, it's painful watching Brian run around the bases. Want to pinch-run?"

"Will this be the fun part?"

Toby called time, and I took Brian's place on first base.

Everybody was talking it up at the top of their lungs.

Toby hit a grounder and got thrown out at first, but I made it all the way to third.

Jason was up at bat. Everyone on the field backed up about ten feet.

"Score or you're dead meat, Matisse." Sam had his fist in the air.

"Let's crush these crybabies!" Brian screamed.

Cooper threw a wild pitch off to the left. It ricocheted off the backstop and rolled almost all the way up to first base.

My team was hollering, "Matisse, steal home!" "Move your butt!" "Steal!" "Steal!" "Steal!"

My legs froze at first, but then I ran. I was stealing. Again. Like at the museum. "I don't want to steal!" I sprinted back to third.

"What!" "Matisse, steal home!"

That was dumb. I took off from third again, heading for home plate. But I stopped halfway there.

"Run, you moron!" they hollered.

"Sorry!" I yelled back. "It was a mistake!"

"Matisse, you big wuss!" "Big chicken!" "Steal!"

"I don't want to steal! I hate stealing!" I yelled at the top of my lungs.

Cooper ran over to me with the ball and touched me. "Out!"

Everybody on my team wanted to kill me except maybe Toby.

Maybe.

And that was only the first inning.

13

After school the next day, I skipped the park—anything would be better than that. I went to the museum and got my ID badge from Prudence.

"Guess what?" Prudence said.

"I'm kind of in a hurry."

"My son is coming for a visit," Prudence said anyway. "I've told him about you." Her body was listing to the left.

"Oh, that's nice." I grabbed her arms and she straightened out.

"Did I ever tell you what he does for a living?"

"No."

"Well, sit for a minute and let's talk."

"I can't right now." I positioned a stool behind her and backed her onto it. "Maybe later."

"I'm looking forward to introducing you. He wants to talk to you about art. Won't that be great?"

"Oh sure. I've got to go. See you later, Prudence," I said, and dashed into the office.

The bulletin board was completely different, and it wasn't in Mom's handwriting anymore. There were columns with dates, times, names, locations, and hours in a graph that looked like hieroglyphics. I should have stayed in the office and studied my vocabulary, but I had to check on my fake first.

People were standing in front of my fake artwork and comparing it to the photo in the museum catalog. It was a stupendous feeling, mixed in with thoughts of who would come to my funeral.

A new guard I had never seen before stood in the room. I didn't see Mr. Snailby. I didn't come for one day, and now something was wrong.

The new guard was tall, and his muscles made ridges on his shirt. His pants were tucked in tight; one hand rested on his baton, the other held a large book. Around his waist was a bulging pack full of gadgets. He walked over to an old man whose toes had crossed a nano-inch over the tape line on the floor. "Back away from the artwork," he snarled.

The old man backed up his walker and touched his heart.

The guard took a deep breath as he removed a

gadget from his belt holster and pushed a few buttons. Then he looked at me. "Do you need assistance, sir?"

"Where is Mr. Snailby?"

"Go to the front desk for information about the former guard of this room."

Former guard? I tore out of the gallery and found Mom in the guards' locker room. She was doing a headstand against the wall.

"My feet feel like dead dogs." Her ugly-quiet shoes were at eye level now.

I had a sinking feeling something bad had happened to Mr. Snailby, or maybe he got blamed for something he didn't do. "Is Mr. Snailby all right?"

Mom dropped her feet and stood up; her face was bright red. "I moved him to another shift."

"I liked being with Mr. Snailby."

"I know, but his legs couldn't take it," Mom said.

"Who's the new guy in the Matisse room?"

"Mr. Bison is the security consultant who is here to observe the operations of our new system. And listen to this"—she grabbed my head in both her hands—"he has worked in the best museums in the world. He orchestrated the security for the *Mona Lisa* at the Louvre in Paris!" Her whole face was smiling.

"Uh-oh," I said.

She released my head. "I'll introduce you." We

took off for the Matisse room. "He's a stickler for rules. He's big, he's focused, and he knows more than I do about art."

We got to the Matisse room.

"Mr. Bison, I'd like you to meet my son, Matisse. Matisse, this is Mr. Bison."

We shook hands and the bones in my fingers snapped like dry twigs.

"Matisse is one of us," Mom said. "He can run around anywhere he likes."

"There is no running in the museum."

"I don't really mean running," Mom clarified. "He mostly sits at his easel."

A beeping sound came out of Mr. Bison's pack. He moved the tranquilizer darts and the fingerprint kit out of the way and fished out the device he'd pushed buttons on earlier. The message SEARCH COMPLETE was flashing red. "This scent detector can decipher fifteen hundred different odors." He pointed at the readout: DRYING OIL-BASE PAINT. He scrolled to the next item: 48 HOURS IN LOCAL ATMOSPHERE. He tore off the printout and handed it to Mom. "Something is freshly painted here," he said, "and I smell something."

Mom bobbed her head up and down. She passed me the printout. "As you know," she said, "most of Van Gogh's paintings are still wet. Only the outside layer of the thick paint is completely dry." She was pleased to demonstrate the scope of her art knowledge. "We have two Van Goghs here."

"This could indicate something serious. There could be altered artwork, defaced canvases."

"If you discover anything unusual," Mom said, "I'll call the police."

"Our new code-red system was completed last night; it calls the police directly. They then deploy officers immediately."

"Excellent," Mom said. "Mr. Bison, Matisse, I'll see you later in the office." Mom took off.

I backed away from Guardzilla while he played with his scent detector. He waited for a couple in matching sweaters to move out of the way, and then he pointed it at the nearest painting. The smell-o-meter stayed at zero. He took short, even steps, keeping the contraption steady in his hands as he pointed it at the center of the next painting.

I careened out of the room to get my easel and paints. When I got back, Mr. Mona Lisa had worked his way around the room, aiming the sniffer at the artwork. He was two paintings away from my wet and smelly *Portrait of Pierre*. I snapped my easel together in front of Pierre and wrenched open my paint box. I unscrewed every tube in the box. I squished long worms of paint onto the palette and waved the palette in the air when he wasn't looking. Seconds later, Mr. Mona Lisa's stink finder was beeping wildly next to my ear.

His face locked in disgust. "My reading is no longer accurate," Mr. Mona Lisa said. He ripped off the printout, which read GROUND ZERO, OIL-BASED PAINT.

I took the paper from him and tried to act innocent. "Oh, oops. This is where I paint."

"You have contaminated the area, and it is impossible to get an accurate reading for seventy-two hours after this kind of exposure." Mr. Mona Lisa banged my easel with his baton. "This is not in compliance with regulations ensuring access for patrons to flow freely through the museum." He showed me a diagram in his rule book, *Museum Guards' Rules and Regulations Magnum Opus*. "Your easel needs to be at a fifty-five-degree angle and your chair legs need rubber booties," he said.

I rearranged my easel as Mr. Mona Lisa watched. He measured it with his protractor, writing calculations in his notebook. Finally, the killjoy initialed a green tag and hung it on my easel. "You are cleared to commence painting."

I went to my locker and got my first two copies of *Portrait of Pierre*, with the mustache and the buckteeth. I set one on my easel, the other one on the floor. I was going to paint over them and exchange one with the masterpiece at home.

That's when Mr. Mona Lisa came back. He was pointing his finger at Section 14 in his manual: "Artwork may be copied, but no caricatures, no humiliating depictions of existing works that . . ."

Mr. Bison was ruining everything.

"Fine. I'm stopping. I'll work on something else." I covered the mustachioed and bucktoothed portraits and wheeled my easel across the room, arranged it in the proper position, and sat down.

I watched Mr. Bison and my fake Pierre. I couldn't paint. I was making zero progress in fixing my big problem. The last thing I wanted to do was copy a different painting. Painting was starting to feel like homework. So I didn't do anything. After sitting awhile, I got it. I got it that I was just a wacko-in-training. I was as cracked as everyone else in my family. My rip-off *Portrait of Pierre* fit right in with the barbecues, Frida's purple problem and bad clothes, and Mom's art obsession. I was more like them than I ever figured. Sure, I could copy masterpieces, but that didn't make me anything. I was a master of nothing. I didn't have any ideas of my own. And I had a blood bond with goofy loons.

On top of that, I was double-dealing everyone in the world—and they were standing in line for it. Hey, everybody, come on in, enjoy! Let me tell you a big fat lie. Talk about smelling bad. Point that stink meter at me and I'll give you a rotten stinky smell: the odor of fried copycat boy.

Mr. Mona Lisa showed me another section in his rule book: "Amateur Artists Must Remove All Equipment at the End of Each Day." He said, "You have five minutes to comply."

Not a problem. I was never going to do artwork ever again. I packed up everything and dropped it off at the locker room. He made me promise to take the humiliating depictions of Pierre out of the museum.

Mr. Mona Lisa walked me all the way to the Security Personnel Office. He stopped with his hand on the doorknob. "Where are you going?"

"I'm allowed in there. Ask my mom."

"That will be reevaluated." Mr. Mona Lisa stared me down while he slowly opened the door. I walked fast to Mom's desk and took a seat.

Rows of gadgets covered the conference table. Mom was reading some papers. She looked up when we came in. "Mr. Bison, what is your team working on this weekend?" Mom asked.

"Heat, humidity, dust, dirt, light, and solar radiation can cause irreparable damage to paintings," Mr. Bison said. He picked up items from the table as he talked. "Temperature gauge controls will be placed and set at sixty-four degrees, along with humidity meters set to 60 percent and light sensors at .02 percent fade factor, and micromesh dust filters will go in all the vents. Also, here's ample inventory of acid-free gloves, tissues and dusting cloths, required for any handling of the collection."

"That's the last of it, then?"

"There's a final seminar on art thievery and vandalism: first response, detaining a suspect, contacting the police, writing a report, testifying in court, and ensuring maximum jail time for the perpetrators."

"Thanks, Mr. Bison."

"Good night." Mr. Bison left the room.

"Mom, can I take some gloves, acid-free tissues, and cloths?"

"Sure. We have an ample supply."

14

Just stealing the painting wouldn't get me into much trouble compared to what would happen if I wrecked the painting. Grounded—what was I thinking? The kind of grounding I'd get would be called doing time in a place called jail. I was going to be behind bars chiseling the days of the week—ten to twenty years' worth—into a concrete wall.

When we got home the garage was open. Dad's car was parked on the lawn, and the back end was weighted down with something heavy. "Matisse. I need a hand."

"In a minute." I hurried to the den, lowered the

lights, closed the windows, set the thermostat to sixty-four degrees, and dusted every surface in the room with an acid-free cloth. Not knowing the humidity had me worried.

I passed Frida in the garage on my way back out front. Her latest creation was pinned on Fridakenstein and she was circling around it hot-gluing doohickeys to it.

Man Ray was out front, busy in his sandbox. Scoopers and digger rigs were all around him. "Play dump trucks?"

"Sorry. I have to help Dad."

"Why?"

"I'm hauling something out of his trunk."

"Why?"

"When you're older you'll understand."

"Why?"

"Because you'll be doing it."

I helped Dad load eighty pounds of coal into his new barbecue. He soaked the coals with two cans of lighter fluid and used a miniblowtorch to set them on fire. He could have sent smoke signals to Argentina.

"Don't go far," he said. "We'll get the wild boar from the trunk when the coals get hot."

"What does a wild boar weigh?"

"She's a well-fed one-hundred-twenty-pounder."

She outweighed me by thirty pounds. "Can't wait, Dad."

I went to my work area in the garage and took a big wooden jewelry box from the bottom shelf. It was old and the top cover had broken off. You could look right into the partitioned rows of squares that probably once held cuff links and necklaces. And unless you knew where to look, you would never see the best part. On the bottom of the box was a hidden drawer that could be opened by pushing a secret spot in the front. The drawer was about three inches high and as big as the whole box in area.

I cut out Mona Lisa's face from an art magazine and fitted it inside one of the squares intended for jewelry. With a dab of Adhere Aplenty and a pushpin, she stayed in place. Twisted and corkscrewed pieces of metal off the garage floor reminded me of trees in a forest, and they looked good inside a square that I painted blue. With a piece of clay, I made a little person, and I put it between the metal trees.

"Hey," I said to Frida. She had been watching me for who knows how long.

"I'm wearing this for my birthday. What do you think? Should I add anything else?" Frida asked.

"I hate it when you spy on me." I stood up to look at her. "What is it?"

"The left half is a little girl's dress and the right half is for a grown woman—which I will be tomorrow when I turn fifteen." She turned to one side. "The past." She turned to the other side. "The present."

"And the purple. Both sides make you look weird."

"Aaaarrrh. Thanks for nothing."

Until I stood up I hadn't noticed that a bunch of people had gathered on our front lawn. Toby wasn't there, but Lizzie and her folks were. Smoke from the barbecue billowed for miles across the sky. Dad was explaining the hugeness of the inferno to the neighbors, and saying that getting boar meat tender came at a price.

Frida went outside in her hand-sewn split personality.

Dad turned and saw me in the garage. "Matisse. I need you now." He waved his meat tongs at me.

I didn't move.

"Matisse," he said again. "I could use your help."

I stayed in the back of the garage.

"Matisse!"

Me lugging a hundred and twenty pounds of croaked boar in front of an audience wasn't going to happen. I got down on the floor under my desk.

Not much time went by before Frida was staring down at me.

"And you think *I'm* weird," she said. "Dad needs you now or the boar will be ruined."

"Why can't we eat hamburgers? I hate your dress—both sides of it."

"I love my dress," Frida said. "And I like Dad's food. Who do you think you are? Get over yourself. Go help Dad."

I kept my eyes on the ground when I walked outside. Dad gave me the scary hooked tongs that required every muscle in my upper body to operate.

The marinating beast inside Dad's trunk had no right to be called a she. I opened the tongs, positioned them, squeezed them shut around the hefty stiff, and lifted. Dad speared her with the spit.

Oohs and ahs came from the crowd.

We maneuvered her into the barbecue.

Everybody clapped.

Dad made an announcement: "Frida wants to invite all of you to her birthday dinner tomorrow night. Payback for tonight's disruption."

Greasy, drippy, and lumpy describes what was all over my clothes when we were done. Getting the smell off my hands would take days. I turned and walked away.

"Matisse," Dad called. "Take the meat tongs into the kitchen for me."

I didn't stop.

Later that night, I went back to the garage because I couldn't sleep. Frida's new fifty-fifty dress was on Fridakenstein. She'd put more buttons on it. They were made from acorns that she took out of my collection. They were spray-painted purple.

15

The next morning, the aroma of barbecuing wild boar filled our house.

No matter how I figured it, big party plus stolen painting equaled disaster. And that would mean me wearing stripes and a number on my back. It had to come off the wall.

I took the wooden jewelry box into the den. I popped opened the hidden drawer. I had lined it with the acid-free tissue. It was big enough to hold Pierre.

Wearing the acid-free gloves, I took *Portrait of Pierre* off the wall and carefully lowered it into the drawer. But before I could close it, Mom came into the room.

"Listen, mister. You hurt your father's feelings last night," she said.

"Mom, we need to talk."

"You need to talk to your dad." She pointed at Pierre. "I want this on the wall for the party tonight. Are you playing museum with the special gloves?" Mom lifted Pierre out of the drawer with her bare hands!

"I'm not playing museum. This is for real. You and I need to talk."

She noticed the squares I had designed. She put her finger in the square with Mona Lisa's face. "I like the pushpin in her eye."

In one move, I took Pierre from Mom and put him back into the drawer. I was out of sneaky ideas. "I want this painting," I said.

"Matisse, you always drum up some drama to get attention away from your sister on her birthday—you started last night."

"Drama? It's a nightmare. You should sit down."

Man Ray ran into the room crying. He had a hair clip stuck on his lip.

Mom squatted down and took the clip off. She picked him up, and he yelped right in her face.

"Mom, this painting!" I had to holler over Man Ray's bawling. "I want it!"

"Shhh, now, now." She stroked Man Ray's hair, but he didn't stop crying.

I didn't want to "just fix it" by myself anymore. "Mom. This is the painting from the museum."

Mom wasn't paying any attention to me. She barely held on to Man Ray when he lurched backward.

"Mom!" I spoke louder. "You're not listening to me."

"What?" She bounced Man Ray up and down.

Man Ray got hysterical.

For effect, I lifted Pierre up and held him in front of Mom and my blubbering brother. "I need help getting this original Matisse back to the museum so you won't lose your job and I won't have to go to jail!" I was screaming. "My stinky copy is hanging in the museum."

Mom's face twisted way over to one side. "Huhhh?" Mom sounded like a horn, and a thin mist of spit flew out of her mouth. "What did you say? I can't hear you."

"Mom, listen to me!"

Dad came into the room and touched Man Ray's cheek. "Now, now."

With them both there it was going to be a lot harder to spill the bad news.

Man Ray's crying got quieter, and he closed his eyes. Mom laid him down on the couch.

Dad had been watching me the whole time. "You and I need to talk."

"I really need to talk to Mom."

Frida came in, holding her new dress in the air. "Mom!" She saw me and pointed. "You ruined my dress!" Frida yelled.

"You purple-ized and used things of mine without asking. I cut them off," I said.

"Aaaarrrh! I hate you!" Frida stormed out of the room.

I put Pierre in the drawer.

"You're going to screw up my system if you move this painting," Mom said. She took Pierre out of the drawer and put him back on the wall. "Enough with the drama. Talk to your father." Mom followed Frida.

"Boy oh boy. You're on a roll," Dad said. "Apparently I'm not the only one disappointed in you."

He had no idea how really disappointing I could be. I wanted our little talk over fast. "I'm sorry about last night. I wanted to hide—that's all—not be here. Sorry."

"Where did you want to be?"

What kind of question was that? I wished Man Ray would get up and start crying really loudly. "I don't know, Dad—the park." I really had no idea.

"If you're sitting here wishing you were at the park, guess what, you're not here *or* at the park. So where are you?"

How did I know? What was he getting at? "I don't know, Dad."

"Your behavior is hurtful. What is going on?"

How could I make him understand without hurting his feelings some more? It was impossible, so I just said it. "I'm embarrassed to be with you. You and Mom and Frida don't care what people think, but I do."

Dad sighed and looked out the window before he answered. "Before I do anything, here's what I think about: Am I helping someone? Am I learning something? Does it make me laugh? Or does it taste good? Here's what I don't think about: What do other people think of what I am doing?"

* * *

I spent the rest of the afternoon in the garage, feeling like the heel of the century. I painted Pierre's face on a small piece of Styrofoam and stuck it in one of the squares of the wooden box.

Then I painted over my other two paintings of Pierre, blotting out the mustache and the buckteeth. I had just finished when Toby walked into the garage.

He plopped down an overnight bag. "Everybody on the block is here, including Lizzie. She couldn't wait to go to a big girl's party." Toby saw Pierre painted on the Styrofoam. "Time out. Matisse, buddy." Toby got serious like I've never seen him before. "You're possessed. Don't be a guy who makes a big mistake that he never lives down. Either get over it or fix it—or it will eat you alive."

"I'm going to swap one of these Pierres with the one on the wall."

"You can't now, your house is full of people. But do something one way or the other. Soon."

Dad stuck his head in the door. "The wild boar sloppy joes are ready. Come out."

"Let's have some fun. Eat cake." Toby pulled me by the arm. "We're going."

In the den, grown-ups were eating from plates on their laps. The kids were outside. Pierre seemed fine above the couch except for the temperature, the draft from outside, the dust being kicked up into the air, and the unknown humidity.

The sliding doors to the backyard were open; Dad was dishing out food. Frida was at the center of a gaggle of girls who were eating and laughing. I saw the back of Lizzie's head.

We walked up to Dad's chow stand. Dad was wearing his puffy white hat, and *Meat Maestro* was scrawled in red Sharpie on his apron. "Eat as much as you can," he said. "There's boar sloppy joes or pizza. Fill out the questionnaire when you're done."

I wanted pizza, but I didn't want to hurt Dad's feelings again. "Boar sloppy, please."

Toby shoveled boar carcass into his mouth. "This is so good."

To me, it tasted like what the soles of my shoes, mixed with mud, might taste like. I wondered if there was such a thing as Mad Wild Boar Disease. After a few bites, something resembling the Olympic torch was burning inside my stomach.

"Matisse, eat and then go find the badminton rackets in the hall closet," Mom said.

Frida waved a broomstick in the air. "Limbo in the den."

"I smell a photo op." Toby fished his cell phone out of his pocket. "I'll get pictures."

"Keep an eye on Pierre—I'll be right back," I said.

Toby gave me the thumbs-up and went into the den.

I took my time digging around in the closet for the rackets.

After a little bit, Toby came out of the den looking for me. "I got some great pictures for all our future blackmail needs." Toby scrolled through the photos. "Look at this. Frida's bent so far back, it doesn't look like she has a head. And Lizzie—I've never seen a wedgie that deep—"

I stared at the picture, not hearing another word he was saying. Then I got up and ran into the den. The wall was bare! Pierre was gone!

Splat! Sploosh! Came from outside, followed by loud cheering.

We ran outside.

Splat! Splew!

Splat! Sploosh!

I saw Pierre, all three of him.

Frida saw me and stuck her tongue out. Then she cracked up.

The paintings were hanging on our back fence. The girls were lined up ten feet away from the paintings, throwing water balloons at them. Balloons were exploding and big wet circles dotted the fence. Luckily, it didn't look like anybody had a good arm. Where was Mom, the painting ayatollah, when I needed her?

Toby gripped my shoulder. "You need to get that painting right now, buddy."

Lizzie was at the front of the line, aiming a balloon right at the paintings.

"Bad news, Lizzie pitches for her softball team," Toby said.

"Lizzie! No!" I said sharp and loud. "Lizzie! Do not throw that balloon!"

Lizzie snapped her head in my direction. Our eyes locked.

"Stop!" I said louder, and pointed at her. "Put it down. Now!" Lizzie was not going to ruin my life anymore.

I marched to the fence, glowering at Lizzie the whole way. I took the masterpiece off the fence while everybody watched. I passed Mom, who was carrying a two-tiered purple sponge cake all lit up with candles.

"Happy birthday, Frida," Mom said.

I left with Pierre and found a place to hide for the rest of the night.

16

I woke up the next morning in the closet where I had gone to hide. Pierre was cradled in my lap on a bed of acid-free tissue, exactly where he was when I fell asleep. The closet door was open, and Toby was snoring halfway out into the hall. The tail of his shirt was in his mouth.

The doorbell rang. As parents arrived, Mom ushered girls out the door. When she came through the hall, she nudged Toby with the tip of her slipper. "Everybody out," she said. "Party's over."

I had slept with my shoulders bent around a canoe paddle and a hockey stick. I hadn't moved all night. The only feelings I had in my limbs were sharp, prickly needles.

Lizzie came by the closet and stood over Toby. She leaned in and smiled at me. "How'd you sleep?"

"Everything hurts. Other than that, I'm good."

"Well," she said, "you look pretty stupid in the back of the closet."

I wasn't in the mood to take any lip from Lizzie. I wanted her to go away. "Bye, now," I said.

But she didn't go away. She just stood there until she finally said, "It's kind of cool that you're an artist."

That was a first, Lizzie saying anything nice to me. I didn't trust her one little bit. "Oh, really?"

"Yeah." Lizzie looked down at the used socks she had in her hands. Then she said, "I wish I could make things like you do."

That surprised me too. "Yeah, right."

"Like those paintings," she said.

"What about the paintings?"

"I wouldn't have thrown a water balloon at them even if you hadn't screamed at me. Especially the good one."

"Good one?" I asked her.

"The one that's better than the other two, the one with . . ." Lizzie was thinking. "The one with . . . something. The one in your lap."

I couldn't believe it. Lizzie, of all people, could see it.

"Lucky for you"—Lizzie pointed at Pierre in the painting—"I didn't throw my knuckleball and hit you in the kisser."

I held up Pierre to face Lizzie. I talked in a squeaky voice as I bobbed him up and down. "A knuckle job in my kisser? Oh, no thanks."

Lizzie and I both laughed really hard.

"Talk to me sometime. When you're not too busy painting yourself over and over again."

We both laughed really hard again.

Lizzie dropped her socks on Toby's face and walked away.

Toby sat up. "Did I just hear that?"

"I think so," I said.

Toby dragged himself up and out the door. After everybody else slumped out of our house, and I had some feeling back in my legs, I took Pierre to my room.

* * *

It was Sunday, and all day at our house, no one got dressed. Every now and then Mom would clean something up, or Dad would do something manly in the garage, or Frida would try on one of her many birthday presents. But all in all, lying down was the position of choice. The phones were unplugged, the drapes were closed, and we were all just ships passing in the night for the entire day. And even though

Man Ray was the only one who got to bed on time the night before, he too was enjoying our cavelike behavior. Up in our room.

I leaned Pierre up on the pillows of my bed, and I told Man Ray everything. Man Ray was a good listener. I told him how I got the painting, and that I might go to jail if anything happened to it. Man Ray didn't judge me or make me feel bad. He laughed when I put on the striped shirt that matched the one Pierre was wearing. He looked worried when I told him about the water balloons. He was mad that Mr. Mona Lisa knew about the wet paint. And he looked sad when I told him Mom could lose her job over something like that.

"Man Ray, I need to return this painting."

"Mine."

"Not yours. Not mine. It belongs to the world."

We both sat quietly, looking at the masterpiece. It had something, like Lizzie said. You could feel it. Mine was painted from my elbow down. The real one came from someplace deep inside Henri Matisse.

"Take my advice, Man Ray. Make something of your own. Don't copy what other people do, or you won't have anything to call yours. Make your own mistakes. And don't do what I do, do what I say." I was starting to sound like an old man.

The *Portrait of Pierre* story had made both of us tired, so Man Ray and I snuggled up together and took a long nap.

As it turned out, my nap was longer than Man

Ray's. Because when I woke up, Man Ray was playing with the painting on the bed, trying to get Pierre to open his mouth and suck on his pacifier.

And when I started to remind Man Ray about the story of Pierre, I realized it would just be safer to watch Man Ray like a hawk until I could get my annoying problem out of the house.

So when Man Ray wasn't looking, I slipped Pierre under my bed.

Man Ray and I spent the rest of the afternoon down in the garage. He sat next to me at my desk coloring while I decorated more squares in the top of the wooden box. In one, I lined the walls with the DRYING OIL-BASED PAINT printout from Mr. Mona Lisa. In a new square, a row of toothpick prison bars trapped Toby's small ball inside it. In another square, deflated water balloons looked like sleeping bats after I'd hung them upside down. One of Mom's old security name tags made me smile when it was fitted with a frame I made out of clay.

The day went fast. I had many more ideas than I had time. When it was dark, I took the box up to my room and lowered Pierre into the secret bottom drawer with the acid-free tissue. He could spend the night there. He was safe.

Tomorrow I'd take Pierre to school and hide him in my locker until I could take him to the museum. Then, Pierre's sleepover field trip would really be over.

17

The next morning it was pouring. It wasn't just droplets; it was a blowing, sideways rain. My life was a perfect storm, and now it matched the weather. There was no way I could take the painting outside.

I screamed into my pillow, and when I looked up, Man Ray had my box and had taken Pierre out. For a minute I didn't care, until I saw two glistening snail trails coming out Man Ray's nostrils. He cocked his head back.

I scampered across the floor on my knees and pinched my fingers over his nose and mouth and snatched the painting out of his hand. When I let go,

Man Ray blew a splattering sneeze in the air that shot disease shrapnel everywhere.

"Man Ray, can you say 'My brother is in jail'?" I asked, as I put Pierre back in the box.

"Pierre all gone?" Man Ray burped.

"I wish Pierre all gone. But Pierre still here."

Mom stuck her head in the door. "Full rain gear today."

"Pierre all gone, Mommy," Man Ray said.

I put my hand over Man Ray's mouth.

Mom pushed into the room. "What on earth, Matisse? Are you playing some kind of don't-let-your-brother-breathe game?"

I lifted off my slippery hand and gave Man Ray a you-better-shut-up look. Of course, that didn't work.

"Please, Matisse. Wash your hands!"

"Pierre all gone," Man Ray said again.

Mom picked Man Ray up. "Who's Pierre?"

"Mommy's job all gone."

"I have a job. I love my job."

"Pierre all gone. Mommy's job all gone." Man Ray started to cry.

She pressed her lips to his forehead. "Are you getting sick? You sound delirious. Let's blow your nose, and then we'll have Dad's beef du jour."

They left me alone in the room. Alone except for His Annoyance, sitting inside the drawer of my decorated box. I was starting to really hate him. How had things gotten so bad so fast?

I opened the drawer, and Pierre and I had a talk. "Am I going to be able to have a regular day at school and forget about you, or am I going to need a moat with alligators, or guards perched on the roof today? Huh? Sure, you're a one-of-a-kind irreplaceable item, but you are on your own. No more special treatment. There won't be any more hiding places or human shields from every greasy, wet, exploding thing that seems to find its way to you. You are a very demanding and seriously spoiled person. You're going to have to stay one more day, and believe me, I'm not happy about it either. So quit snarling and pouting and acting all superior, because as far as I know, you aren't even a real guy; you're just one-dimensional and that puts me on top, doesn't it?"

Pierre didn't say anything.

"Yeah. Nice talking to you too."

I closed the drawer and left the box right on top of my dresser. I went to school.

18

Later, at the museum, something was definitely going on. The parking lot was full, and I had to wait on line in the rain just to get in the front door. When I got to the reception desk, Prudence wasn't there. Another volunteer was helping.

"Where's Prudence?" I asked.

"She's giving a private tour," the volunteer said. "A very important person is here."

The main corridor was packed with more people than normal getting brochures and heading to the exhibits. I wasn't happy to be faking out a whole bunch more people with my phony artwork. I'd rather stick my finger in a wall socket.

I dropped my stuff off and headed down the hall to the east gallery and the Matisse room. When I got there, Mr. Mona Lisa was at the entrance.

"Stop. I need to detain you." Mr. Mona Lisa used his baton to block me from going into the room.

"Detain me?"

"Matisse!" I heard from behind me. Prudence stood about fifteen feet away. Next to her was a humongous police officer.

"That's him." Prudence pointed at me.

The police officer pointed his finger too, but his looked like a gun.

Was he coming for me? I didn't stop to think. I dove under Mr. Mona Lisa's baton and started running for the exit across the room, dodging people as I went. I took one last look behind me before I turned the corner.

I didn't want to get arrested right in the middle of the museum in front of all these people.

I ran like a gazelle, zigzagging in and out of galleries and down hallways. I hauled butt through every wing of the museum. When I was sure I had completely lost Prudence and the cop, I made a beeline for the front door. But I didn't make it.

"There he is! Matisse!"

I did an about-face and ran the other way.

"Please stop!" they yelled.

I stepped on it. This time I headed past the

Matisse room to the back of the museum, all the way to the security guards' locker room. No one was there. I walked around the bank of lockers and sat down to catch my breath. I was sucking in big gulps of air when I heard the door open.

I couldn't see who it was. A locker clanked open.

I heard buttons being pushed on something mechanical.

"Monday. Coffee break number five." It was Mr. Mona Lisa talking into a recorder. "Large crowd at museum. Matisse ran through exhibit. Did not respond to subliminal halt whistle."

I had to hide. There was no other choice but to open a locker and step inside it. By reducing my size and making round places on my body turn square, along with resting my nose on a hook, I was able to fit.

Through the locker door I heard someone else come into the room.

"Have you seen Matisse?" It was Prudence's voice.

"Not since he ran away," Mr. Mona Lisa answered.

"I need to find him." It was the policeman.

"Sir, I'll search the museum and subdue him," Mr. Mona Lisa said.

I wasn't sure what it meant, but being subdued by Mr. Mona Lisa didn't sound good. I waited awhile for everybody to leave. Then I busted out of the locker.

There was a service elevator in the back of the room. The doors were open, and I got in. The basement was the only other floor on that elevator, but I didn't want to go there because it would be dark. I smashed the CLOSE DOOR button and held it down. I would have stayed until the museum closed, but a loud buzzer went off, and a plastic cover popped off a switch that read PULL FOR FIRE DEPARTMENT.

I released the CLOSE DOOR button and backed into a corner. Then the doors parted. The buzzing stopped. Five seconds later the doors closed. They opened and closed, opened and closed. The elevator could feel my weight. The next time the doors closed, I spread my legs and swung my feet up onto the handrail and leaned my back into the corner. The doors stayed closed. It worked. "Ha-ha."

"Matisse. What are you doing?" The voice came out of nowhere.

"Who's there?" I tried not to sound scared.

"It's Ms. Whitsit, in the control booth. I see you, and you're setting off all kinds of bells and whistles on my console."

I looked up. The ceiling security camera was pointed right at me.

"Matisse," Ms. Whitsit said. "Get off the railing and stop playing around."

"I need to . . ."

"Get out of the elevator," she said. "There's a police officer—"

I darted out of the elevator, through the locker room, and back into the museum.

It was less crowded than before. I didn't see Prudence or the policeman.

I had to go by the Matisse room to get out. There was a sign: MATISSE EXHIBIT CLOSED. Plastic was draped over the doorway. I peeked around it to look. Crates were stacked in the corner. Some paintings were off the wall. My fake wasn't there! They closed the exhibit because of the missing masterpiece!

I ran for the exit and didn't stop. I almost got out, but Mr. Kramer grabbed my arm and pulled me back inside.

"Come with me." Mr. Kramer dragged me to the door of the auditorium. "In here." He opened the door. He pointed into the darkened room. "Get in there. It's starting."

"But I—"

"I told them I'd get you. Now get in there."

19

I stepped inside the auditorium and Mr. Kramer closed the door behind me.

It was dark, but I could see the outlines of people sitting in the seats. The place was full. A single beam of light lit up a podium in the middle of the stage. The stage curtains rustled as a man stepped out from behind them. He was slightly bent over and he walked at half speed toward center stage. As he got closer, his suit fabric shimmered. His socks were red. He reached the podium and took a few moments to catch his breath. Wrinkles lined his face and his hair was thinning. He was old. His face was in shadow, but when he lifted his chin and the light shone on his eyes, I knew.

The old man began to speak with a French accent. "My name is Pierre Matisse. My papa was Henri Matisse."

Everybody clapped.

All the blood drained out of my body. The Pierre from the painting—him, it, my big problem—was standing right there. In person, a much older person, but still right there. I moved my hands over my mouth just in time to stop *Oh-no-oh-no-oh-no-oh-no-oh-no* from spilling out.

A large screen came down from the ceiling and a painting appeared on it.

Old Pierre began his talk. "When my papa first started painting . . ."

Pierre was speaking, but soon I couldn't make out a word he was saying. I watched his lips shaping words, but I could only hear the sound of my teen years being chipped away one at a time. One after the other, images of his father's paintings were displayed on a large screen and words were said. And then—and then—there it was: my big problem, *Portrait of Pierre*. High on the screen, enlarged in PowerPoint, Pierre's face, huge and serious, loomed over me along with the moment of truth. My ears popped like stretched balloons, as if I had fallen into Earth's atmosphere from a thousand miles up.

Pierre's voice was booming now.

"A painting should be a unique thing, a birth, showing something new to the world, *n'est-ce pas?* An artist's paintings are a declaration of who he is."

His words broadcast directly to my insides, skipping skin and hair and hitting my innermost atoms, rearranging them all.

"A truly original artist," Pierre went on, "invents his work from the world around him and mostly from the world inside his heart."

He must know about the missing painting.

Pierre gestured toward his portrait on the screen. "This is my favorite painting, *bien sûr.* I remember everything about the day *mon père* decided to paint my portrait. We had guests, and I was sitting at one end of a long table set for lunch. My papa gazed at me for a while, drinking in the light and colors. I had sparked his imagination. He painted me while the others enjoyed lunch. I felt important. It is my favorite painting for so many reasons." The hunched and very old Pierre stepped around the podium and looked up at his enlarged portrait for a long time.

What had I done? Stinging guilt ricocheted through my veins. Each breath felt like hot lava. I had stolen from this nice old man. I was a big cheater, a faker, a lousy no-good thief.

I slunk out of the auditorium, and I told Mr. Kramer to tell the policeman that I was waiting outside. The police car wasn't locked. I opened the door and got in.

26

Shortly thereafter, the policeman came down the steps two at a time, cupped his face on the window, and glared at me. "You're a tough fella to catch," he said, climbing in.

"I'm done running," I said. "You can take me in now."

"Take you in?"

"You can book me, or send me to the torture chamber, whatever you want."

He looked puzzled. "Oh . . . I get it, the running. You've been playing cops and robbers. I did the same thing when I was your age, and heck, I'm still doing it, except now I'm the one doing the chasing." He laughed. "I'm Chief John McGuire. Pretty cool, huh? Do you want to wear my hat for a minute?"

Wear his hat? "No, sir. I'd rather not drag this out. I'd like to go to headquarters now."

"I need to talk to you," he said.

We both knew I swiped the masterpiece. What else was there to talk about? "Sir, is there any way you could drive away from the museum, and then we could talk?"

Chief McGuire wrinkled his forehead.

"Or we could just go?" I said. "I'm ready. At the station I get one phone call, right?"

"Criminals get one phone call," he said.

"What about art thieves?"

"Yes, I suppose they do."

"I'll call my mom from there. Just so you know, my mother is innocent."

"I'm a little lost here. But speaking of mothers, mine speaks very highly of you. She thinks you're an artistic genius or something."

"Your mother?"

He pointed to Prudence, who was standing on the other side of the glass doors to the museum. She saw us looking her way and blew us a kiss. "I thought she told you I was coming," he said. "I like to paint in my spare time, and I was hoping you could give me a few pointers."

"About art? You've been chasing me all over the museum so you could get a few pointers?"

A snapping noise came out of the dashboard radio. "Chief McGuire, do you read me?"

The chief reached forward and pushed a button. "McGuire here. Yes, I read you."

"What is your ETA at headquarters, sir? The youth-crime-and-lethal-punishment seminar is about to begin. Over."

"I'll be there in five. Over."

"Copy that."

The chief shook his head. "It's too bad I had to spend so much time chasing you. I would have enjoyed talking to you about art, but now I have to go. Can I drop you somewhere?"

"How about off a cliff."

"Ha-ha." He stuck the key in the ignition. "You'll need to get out of the car, Matisse. I have to get going."

What was I supposed to do now? Whenever I felt like confessing, nobody wanted to listen. "So that's it?" I said. "You're going to headquarters and I'm free to go?"

"Yep." He reached into the glove compartment and handed me a plastic badge and a pair of ugly sunglasses. "If you step out of the car I have something else you'll really like."

I slithered onto the sidewalk, in the pouring rain.

Chief McGuire turned on the flashing lights and siren. *Eeeuuuuuooooowhopwhopwhop.* And then, to top it off, over the loudspeaker he said, "Matisse, you are under arrest. Put your hands in the air." He waited a few seconds, then added, "Just kidding." He laughed into the microphone. "Pretty cool, huh?" He peeled out with the siren blaring at the same moment a large truck pulled in. On the side was printed WE MOVE EXPENSIVE ART.

I knew what I had to do. I didn't care what happened to me anymore. So what if I was the kid with the ankle detector who cleaned the freeway on weekends?

I had to get the painting back to Pierre.

21

I ran home. Nothing could stop me, not even the downpour slapping my face. *Portrait of Pierre* was going back to the museum no matter what.

The hill of our cul-de-sac had become a flowing river. I saw Toby banging on his window, waving me into his house. I kept running.

Nobody was home when I got there. I flew up the stairs into my room, and opened the drawer in the wooden box. Pierre was resting inside.

"We have to talk." I leaned Pierre up so I could look him in the eyes. "Can't say I'm sorry it's over or that it was great having you, because really, the sooner you're gone, the better. We've had a few adventures I'll never forget as long as I live, but you really need to go now. You turned out to be a very nice old man and I don't want to make you sad. And this outlaw life I'm living right now is not for me. I want it over. Let's just say goodbye and we'll do what we have to do and move on. So, goodbye." And I closed the drawer.

There was one unfinished square on top of the box. I stuck my new police badge sideways into the empty space.

The doorbell rang. It was Toby.

"I've come to help," he said as he stepped inside. "Your mom called and asked if you were at my house. I figured something must be up. So here I am."

"What did you tell her?"

"I didn't say you were actually at my house, I just said you were . . . around. And she said okay, bye. And I figured you must be up to something that . . . you know . . . you don't want her to know about. So I'm helping you. That's all."

I grabbed Toby's arms and shook him. "Listen, the last thing I want is for you to get into trouble for something I did. I'm the guilty one, not you; you've just been a really good friend to me, that's all. Besides, who's going to get my missed homework assignments when I'm . . . when . . . ? Well, you know."

"If you put it like that."

Toby followed me into the kitchen. I got a roll of

plastic bags and some duct tape to protect the painting from the rain. "Since you're still here, take these. I'll be right back."

I hurried up the stairs to get Pierre. I opened the drawer one last time. "This is it. Let's go."

Pierre was ready.

On the way downstairs there was a distinct smell of plastic.

"Toby?" I didn't see him anywhere. Maybe he decided to leave after all. "Hey, Toby?"

"I'm in the bathroom," Toby said. "I'll be right out."

"Don't be long. I've got to do this right now."

Toby shot out of the bathroom. "What's that smell? I hope it's not . . ." Toby led me around the couch. The roll of plastic bags was on the floor heater grate. The duct tape was sitting on the grate too.

"Toby!"

"Yikes!" Toby lifted the bags off the grate and then dropped them right away. "Wow, that got hot fast."

I picked up the tape. It was just hot enough to have fused the tape to itself.

"I have more bags at my house," Toby said.

"There's no time." I fished out two umbrellas from the hall closet. I started to push one open.

"That's bad luck," Toby said.

"I have to see if it works."

"Yeah, but, it's bad luck to open it inside."

"Things couldn't get any worse, could they?" I pushed open the umbrella. It was fine for a few seconds, and then on its own it continued to open up until it turned into a tulip facing the ceiling. "Shoot."

"Told you it was bad luck."

I started to open the other one, but Toby grabbed it out of my hands and stepped outside. It worked fine. Except it was only big enough to cover someone between the ages of two and three.

"We have to think of something else," I said.

"Why don't we get a bunch of Man Ray's diapers and wrap them around the box and run really fast," Toby said.

"I have another idea." I looked out the window at Dad's barbecues locked up on the porch.

"No way!" he said.

"Way."

Toby smiled like a jack-o'-lantern.

The wild boar barbecue was too big. The chicken barbecue was too small. But the pig barbecue was just right. And besides, I had pushed that one before.

I got the pig barbecue keys out of the drawer and rattled them in the air. I performed my best imitation of Mom. "I hope you brought your driver's license." And Toby and I both laughed really hard.

We took a bunch of towels from the bathroom. We wrapped Pierre's box in one towel and used the rest to pad the inside of the barbecue. We closed the hood and then strapped a flashlight to the top to help us see where we were going.

I unlocked the barbecue from the railing.

It was raining worse than before. Getting the brown bomb off the porch and through the gate was harder than it looked. The moment I pushed the thing into position facing down the hill, there was no stopping it from rolling.

Toby was caught off guard. "I didn't hear you say go."

"I didn't. It just started."

"Okay, Captain." Toby saluted me.

On the second half of the hill the barbecue picked up speed.

"You should slow up!" Toby hollered from be-hind me.

"No kidding." I leaned back into the hill. My Converse sneakers were big on style, but the bottoms had about as much traction as a sheet of plastic. For every rotation of the wheels, I took ten braking steps to keep up. The barbecue hurtled down the hill like a giant boulder.

"Get in front! Help me slow it down!" I hollered.

"Ten-four, good buddy." Toby sprinted alongside the barbecue and then passed it. When he was in position, he cut in front.

Meanwhile I slapped both my feet flat on the ground. My shoes became water skis.

"Now what?" Toby screamed over his shoulder.

"Lean back and grab the barbecue!"

Toby flashed me a thumbs-up and went into action. He cooled his pace and let the barbecue catch him. He laid his back on the hull and gripped the sides of the barbecue and dug his heels into the pavement.

I've had worse ideas, but I couldn't think of one.

"Matisse! Help!"

If that brown bomb didn't start angling to the left soon, Toby was going to become one with the hedge at the bottom of the hill.

I leaned all my weight to the left; water fishtailed off my shoes like we were on a lake. "Toby! Hang on!"

"Aaaaahhhhhhhhh!" Toby pulled his feet off the ground and positioned his bent legs up in front of his body to be his bumper.

We careened off the hedge at twenty-five miles per hour. The stop sign four houses away was getting closer. Fast.

My body was bouncing so hard I thought my face would rattle right off. We stopped going straight and started spinning our way to the stop sign. We finished our spinout one house away from the stop sign, facing backward.

Toby jumped off, hopped around for a few seconds, and then slammed down an imaginary football. "Eeeeehhhhaaaa. I think you just saved my life, man."

"Yeah, Toby, I did."

"You're my best buddy, Matisse."

"You're my best buddy too. Help me straighten this out."

We pointed the barbecue toward the museum; the road was flat and the building was only a quarter of a mile away.

We were quiet for a little. Then Toby said, "You're good now, right, Art Man?" He turned to go. "Well, I'll see you. Right?"

"Sure, we'll talk."

"See you, Art Man."

The barbecue behaved itself the rest of the way, but by the time I got to the museum, the building was closed. A few cars were leaving. One of them was Mom's. She didn't see me.

A closed museum was not going to get in my way. There was always someone around; they'd just have to let me in. I pushed the barbecue around to the staff entrance and parked it under the overhang. I took off my wet jacket.

I held my breath and opened the cover. A little water had seeped into the sides of the barbecue. The box hadn't moved. I took it out of the barbecue. Everything was dry and clean and perfect.

22

I banged on the back door of the museum for a few minutes.

Finally, a voice came from inside. "The museum's closed."

"I have to get in. It's important."

"Who's there?"

"It's Matisse."

"It's Mr. Snailby. Your mom just left."

So that was where Mr. Snailby went—the night shift, so he wouldn't have to stand up so much.

"How are your legs?" I asked.

"Well, I made it. I'm retiring. Tonight's my last night."

"It's my last night too," I said. "Can you open up?"

"I'm not allowed to let anyone in," Mr. Snailby said.

"But it's . . . me."

It was quiet for a few seconds. I rested my cheek on the door. "I've done something, Mr. Snailby." I confided through the metal. "There's something I need to tell you. But you have to let me in."

I had lied to Mr. Snailby to get him out of the Matisse room while I tried to fix everything. I was asking Mr. Snailby to do something wrong again. It didn't feel so good, asking him. "Never mind. Forget it, Mr. Snailby. You don't have to. I understand."

I had to think of another way to return Pierre's favorite painting. I turned to go, but keys clanked on the other side of the door. Then the door shook as the locks were being unlocked and the metal bar was slid across.

Mr. Snailby opened the door. He looked at the wooden box in my arms. "What's going on?"

"It's hard to explain. Are you going to be here for a while?" I asked.

"All night," he said.

"I need to hurry."

"You're not going to touch any of the artwork," are you?"

I'd never do that again. "No. They mean too much to people," I said.

Mr. Snailby thought for a second. "Get moving, then."

"I'll tell you everything when I get back." I hurried past him.

In the museum, I saw light bleeding into the hall from the Matisse room. I bolted down the hall. The Matisse room was empty, really empty, except for a man driving a miniforklift loaded with boxes.

"Hey, you're not supposed to be in here." His voice was gruff. "We closed two hours ago."

I dashed out of the room.

"The exit's the other way," he bellowed after me.

Sounds were coming from the loading dock. I raced there. Pierre—Monsieur Pierre—was on the ramp, heading to the exit. A man supported him as he walked. Pierre had my painting in his hand.

Two large men were arranging crates and strapping them down inside the truck. Past the truck was a fancy black car with the doors open, and three people were standing nearby.

Pierre labored down the ramp with his head tipped down. Wisps of white hair fluttered with each step.

I went down the ramp, easily catching up to him. He and the man with him were speaking French to each other, probably talking about my fake. I stepped around in front of them. I was panting like a dog.

I didn't know if I should spit it right out, and just tell Pierre, *It's me, I stole your painting.* And this guy could catch Pierre before he hit the floor from shock. Or if I should break it to him slowly, after he sat down.

"May I help you?" the man asked in a heavy French accent.

"I'd like to talk to Mr. Pierre Matisse."

"*Oui?*" Pierre said to me, and then gestured for the man to go.

They spoke, and the man pointed to his watch before walking back into the museum.

"Yes?" Pierre said to me.

"Oh, ummm . . . Sir." I stuck my hand out. "Hi . . . Ummm, I'm Matisse."

"*Pardon?*" he said.

"That's my name, Matisse, after your dad. Pretty nutty. My mom named me after your dad."

"Your mom?" He thought for a moment. "Ah, *oui*, Sue, the security chief. *Oui, oui*, she told me all about you. Matisse, Man Ray, Frida—*très amusant*. I am Pierre." He shook my hand, leaned in, and squinted. "I used to have a shirt like that."

I was in another striped shirt.

Pierre lifted up my *Portrait of Pierre*. "*Voilà.*" He pointed at his striped shirt in the painting.

"Ahhh . . . yeah. Well . . . that's . . . It's funny you should . . . *voilà* that, because that is exactly what I want to talk to you about."

Pierre held up the painting next to my face just as

135

a revolt erupted in my stomach. He squinted again at me, then looked back at the painting.

My face jerked and twitched. "Of course you know about the painting." I watched for his reaction. He was remarkably calm. "What you don't know is that it was . . . me."

He was taking the news very well. No anger showed in his eyes. He just stared at me. "It's more than the shirt that is the same," he finally said. Pierre studied every corner of my face. "*Remarquable*. Your face, it's as if I am looking at myself as a boy."

"Yes, the name . . . the face . . . the fake. What are the odds?" I rambled.

"Well, *mon ami*, you can only figure you will look like me when you are an old man too." Pierre laughed. "You are looking in the mirror seventy-five years from now." He stuck his face forward. He laughed harder. "You like?"

"I like." His happy old smile made me smile, but just for a second. I had to start confessing about the rest of the story before my insides became part of the permanent collection at the museum. But before the words found their way out, he noticed my box.

"*Magnifique*. May I?" He took my box to a makeshift table near the truck and viewed the open squares I had designed. He bent down low over it. He laughed and pointed at his little portrait on the piece of Styrofoam, he liked the Mona Lisa with the push-pin, he tapped the badge with his knuckle, and he admired the miniature jail cell. "Who is the artist of this box?"

"Oh, that's . . . just me," I said.

"I need my glasses." Pierre handed my fake Matisse painting to me. "Careful, hold it by the sides, *s'il vous plaît*. I never let them crate this painting when the exhibition travels, *très important*."

He removed his glasses from his shirt pocket and nudged them up his nose. Now I understood why he was so calm. He didn't know the painting he passed to me was a fake, because he hadn't actually *voilà*'d it with his glasses on.

I had to start all over again. And if I said another word that wasn't part of fessing up, I'd be a liar and a coward.

"Pierre, sir, I have to confess something. I did a dumb criminal thing—with something of yours, actually. This painting, as a matter of fact." I bobbed my painting up and down. I poked the back of it with my finger. "This painting isn't real. As crazy as that sounds, this isn't the portrait your father painted. You'll see now that you have on your glasses."

"Comment?" Pierre adjusted his glasses, looked at the painting. *"Non . . ."* He looked confused.

I tried to explain. "And things went so bad so fast, but anyway, I painted this one, yeah, it felt good for a minute, but anyway, that's not important. What I want to tell you is—I have the real painting. That's the main part of the bad part." As I spoke, the fake loosened in the frame from my poking it, and before I could stop it, the painting fell out of the frame, face down on the concrete.

"Aaahhh!" Pierre quivered. He stooped over but couldn't bend low enough to pick up the painting.

"That's not the original. It's okay, Pierre."

He snapped his head toward me in a panic. *"C'est une catastrophe!"* hissed from between his teeth.

"No, no, please don't be upset. That's not the masterpiece! *Voilà.*" I pointed at the back of the painting. "See, look, the words your father wrote to you are not there. '*J'adore Pierre. Papa Matisse*'— not there."

I picked the painting up off the floor. "It was a stupid thing to do, I know. But I painted this one. It's a copy."

It was as if smoke were shooting out Pierre's ears now. "Where is my painting?" he demanded.

"I have it. It's safe." I set the frame and the fake on the table and popped open the drawer in the box. The original portrait was nestled inside.

Pierre was aghast. "What have you done?"

"I copied your portrait at the museum. I put my painting in the frame and took yours out. I didn't mean for yours to be out so long, but the alarms weren't working and then they were . . ."

"What?" He gripped the end of the table. His breathing came in short bursts as he hovered over the masterpiece. He started at the top of the painting and worked his way down, scrutinizing every inch.

"And then the security people came and I couldn't switch them back. Your painting ended up at my house—not really on purpose—which was scary, let me tell you. But at least it didn't get wet at the party, and nobody stepped on it . . ."

Pierre looked at me horror-struck.

I went on reassuring him. "No, no, it's okay! I mean, a few people touched it, and there was a close call with a feather duster, and the humidity was probably way, way off." He was getting paler by the second, so I figured I'd save the details for later. "Sooo, other than that . . ."

He carefully lifted his painting out of the drawer and examined it some more. He turned it around and looked at his father's message on the back. Then he began breathing more freely and color reentered his cheeks.

"I took good care of it."

He laid the original *Portrait of Pierre* on top of the frame. Then he contemplated my face again, but this time he wasn't smiling.

"Does your mother know about this?"

"No, sir."

"Impossible."

"My mom doesn't know anything. Please don't get her fired."

Pierre had our lives in his hands. I could be branded the boy who stole the million-dollar masterpiece and got his mom sacked, or he could have mercy and let us go. He deserved to be mad for the rest of his life if he wanted to, and I wouldn't blame him.

"Someone must tell your mother," he finally said.

"I tried to . . . Yes, sir."

"So here we have three choices: the police can tell her, I can tell her, or you can tell her."

If the son of Henri Matisse told Mom I stole one of his father's paintings, she would spontaneously combust. If the police had to tell her, they would definitely have the mother-and-offspring handcuff set ready to slap on our wrists. "What I did was wrong. I'll do whatever you say."

"Your mother will know the correct punishment for your crime."

I couldn't begin to wrap my mind around what Mom might do. "Yes, sir."

"And I will check to make sure you tell her. You are lucky. I see no damage to the painting, but you have committed a grievous crime, young man!"

"Yes, I took something that belonged to you. I'm sorry I did it. I'm sorry—" I stopped when the man came back from inside the museum and stood next to Pierre.

Pierre banged on the metal siding of the truck. "*Messieurs*, come here *tout de suite!*"

The two large men inside the truck hurried to where we were standing. *"Avez-vous un problème?"*

"Oui. Nous avons un grand problème." Pierre looked at me.

I was going to tell Mom, but he was going to tell these three French thugs.

"Pierre," I pleaded. "It will never happen again. I promise."

Pierre didn't speak for a moment. He continued to look at me when he finally spoke to the men. "This painting is falling out of its frame. It needs to be properly secured."

"Oui, Monsieur." Two of the men walked off with the frame and *Portrait of Pierre*. The other man stayed with Pierre.

"As I said before, you are a lucky boy. Do you know why?"

"Because you aren't going to have me arrested?"

"That. But you are lucky also because you are talented." Pierre pointed to my things on the table. "You should throw this away."

"Yes. I will." I scooped up my painting and the box and walked a few steps to a trash can, ready to throw it all in, but Pierre stopped me.

"Not that."

"What?"

"This." Pierre took my fake out of my hand. "It's a good copy, but it's not art." He tossed it into the trash. "It comes from nowhere inside you." He brushed his fingertips on the things in the wooden box. "This, you should keep."

"Really?"

"*Oui*, because it comes from you." He reached toward me and rested his hand on my heart. "Right here, *oui*? This is what will make your art meaningful. Art from your *coeur*, Matisse."

I looked at my box. Each little compartment was full of things I had collected, cut out, or made, and that I had assembled until they looked right. "From my heart."

"Nothing else will do, then." Pierre held his hand on my heart for a few moments. Then he jabbed his fingertip into my chest. "What's this?"

I looked down.

He flicked his fingers up to my nose. "Got you." He nodded at me and turned to go. "I am a collector of good original artwork; your work is of interest to me. *Au revoir*."

"*Au revoir*," I echoed.

The man helped Pierre walk in the direction of the black car.

Pierre kept walking away, but he waved his hand in the air, the hand that had touched my nose.

Pierre turned something bad into something good. It didn't seem possible. All he did was jab his finger on my chest. He called my box *art*. My heart was in every square. And Pierre saw it.

23

When I finally convinced her I was telling the truth, Mom experienced a major case of nerves. As I retold the ugly details leading up to the million-dollar sleep-over, she wrung her hands, looked at the ceiling, and on occasion shrieked and bobbed back and forth. She said, "You are grounded for the next six months." Then she collapsed into bed.

"No matter how you look at it, you're cooked," Dad told me.

Frida was pleased with herself. "I'm the good child now. Who are you?"

Being grounded didn't bother me. I couldn't wait

to get home from school now. After I finished my homework, I would settle in at my workstation in the garage, surrounded by my collections. With welding tools, sanders and screws, glue, and all the other supplies at my disposal, I was making my own museum. I decorated wooden boxes and other containers, which I called "Voyages." There was one for everybody: Toby, Prudence, Mr. Snailby, Mr. Mona Lisa, Lizzie, members of my family, and, of course, Pierre.

With Mom in mind, I lined a wooden box with security-garb material. Using clay, I made twenty miniature shoes with wings attached, then arranged them in the box, in a forest setting. Inside each shoe was a placard with the name of a famous painting. And on the sides and back of the box, I mounted eyes to watch over everything. Dad's Voyage was inside a small welded oil drum. Ground-up barbecue coals looked just right on the bottom, and the back wall was a driver's license. I made tiny meat hooks out of wire and hung bits and pieces of beef jerky on them. And with Scrabble tiles I wrote, LET'S EAT MEAT.

I was in the middle of some: Frida's box was made to look like the inside of a freezer. The shelves were stocked with shellacked meals done up in purple, and Elvis was on the top shelf lit up with Christmas lights. Inside was a free pass for her to use anything in my collections for her clothes. Man Ray's tin box contained a mountain of colorful gummy bears cupped in the paws of King Kong.

As I built the Voyages, I thought about some of the most embarrassing times I'd lived through with my family. The more I thought about them, the more I realized that those same moments were some of the best ones too. I still wouldn't push one of Dad's barbecues down the middle of the street, but I didn't mind being related to the barbecue-parade people so much anymore.

Of course, Toby wanted to help make his Voyage. We made a papier-mâché mold of his head with his mouth open like a fish, and we dangled bait nearby. We signed it *Toby and Matisse.*

Lizzie started hanging around the garage too. She wasn't as bad as she used to be. She organized an exhibit of my Voyages in the display case in the administration building at school. It was my first one-man show.

Pierre's was simple. I lined a lunch box with my striped shirt and put a small wooden table inside. On the one and only chair I placed a red berry and a miniature painting of his father that I painted myself. And right on the table I put the extra nails from the frame at the museum. When it was finished, I wrapped the whole thing in brown paper and shipped it to Pierre. He wrote me back, saying the lunch box was *très magnifique.*

Underneath Mom's, Dad's, Frida's, and Man Ray's Voyages, in a secret place, I wrote a personal message, just like the real Matisse. I signed them all *I love you. Matisse.* Just in case one day, many years from now, the unthinkable happens, and someone copies them perfectly. Perfectly, that is, except for the most important part.

Author's Note

Matisse on the Loose is a work of fiction, but the story was inspired by a real painting, *Portrait of Pierre Matisse*, by Henri Matisse.

Henri Matisse (1869–1954) was one of the greatest French painters of all time, and a master of modern art. The way Matisse got started in art is kind of funny—and kind of painful. As a young man he was a lawyer, until something unexpected changed his life—and the world of art—forever. He had an attack of appendicitis, and while he was recuperating he was given a box of artist's paints to help pass the time. "The moment I had this box of colors in my hands," he later recalled, "I had the feeling that my life was there." And the rest, as they say, is history.

At twenty-two years of age, Matisse quit the law so that he could study art. He was not a natural artist, and twice he failed the entrance exam to get into art school. To improve his painting skills, just like the character in this book, the real Matisse copied masterpieces in a museum.

Matisse is known for his use of bright colors, bold patterns, and flowing lines. He worked hard to keep his paintings simple.

Matisse had two sons and a daughter. The younger son, Pierre (1900–1989), became one of the most influential art dealers in New York. *Portrait of Pierre* was painted in 1909, when Pierre was nine years old. It's not one of Matisse's best works, but it had personal value for Pierre, who was depicted in only two other paintings by his father. The portrait was in Pierre's private collection until he died at the age of eighty-nine. The portrait has been loaned to museums for retrospective exhibitions of his father's work.

Pierre died in 1989, but he is a prominent character in the novel, which is set in the present day so that it can include the latest high-tech security systems.

About Art Heists

Even though it seems almost impossible to imagine how a painting could be stolen from a museum, it happens more often than you might think. Thieves outsmart security systems—climb in windows, drop down from skylights, hide in closets—and sometimes they come in broad daylight and take paintings right out from under everyone's nose. Canvases are cut out of frames and stuffed under coats, paintings are taken at gunpoint, and forgeries are bought and sold as originals. Eighty percent of all art thefts are inside jobs. There are twenty-five thousand works of art listed as stolen, including one hundred and fifty Rembrandts, five hundred Picassos, and many works by Henri Matisse.

Even the most famous painting in the world, Leonardo da Vinci's *Mona Lisa*, was stolen from the Louvre Museum in Paris in 1911. Vincenzo Perugia knew his way around the Louvre because he had helped construct a glass-covered display cabinet for the *Mona Lisa*. He hid in a storage closet, and after the museum had closed, he simply took the painting off the wall and cut it out of the frame. He unscrewed a doorknob on a security door and walked out with the *Mona Lisa* under his shirt. The empty space on the wall the next day didn't cause alarm. The guards had a bad case of *Gee, I thought you had it.* They assumed the *Mona Lisa* was in another part of the museum. Days later they found the empty frame in a stairwell. Perugia kept the painting in his apartment for two years before he got caught trying to sell it to the Uffizi Gallery in Italy. He was sentenced to seven months in jail.

About the Author

Georgia Bragg's father, mother, and brother are all artists, and Georgia is too. She was a printmaker, a painter, and a storyboard artist before becoming a writer. "My parents talked about art seven days a week," she says. "Someone's latest creation was always propped up at the dinner table, so I learned about art by osmosis. I didn't realize how unique my experience was until I got older." Georgia lives in Los Angeles with her husband, two children, and two cats.